Stories of the Unseen

Madiha Khan

Ukiyoto Publishing

All global publishing rights are held by

Ukiyoto Publishing

Published in 2023

Content Copyright ©Madiha Khan

ISBN 9789360492175

All rights reserved.
No part of this publication may be reproduced, transmitted, or stored in a retrieval system, in any form by any means, electronic, mechanical, photocopying, recording or otherwise, without the prior permission of the publisher.

The moral rights of the author have been asserted.

This book is sold subject to the condition that it shall not by way of trade or otherwise, be lent, resold, hired out or otherwise circulated, without the publisher's prior consent, in any form of binding or cover other than that in which it is published.

www.ukiyoto.com

Dedication

This book is dedicated to all the super women who are trying to do it all. Working, taking care of their family and home, sacrificing themselves for others and getting no appreciation from anyone. But these super women smile through it all! You are not alone, we see you, and you are doing great!

Acknowledgement

The idea for this book had been stewing in my mind for a while now. I wanted to write a book about my paranormal experiences but was lacking the drive. During my stewing, I came across some ladies, who had amazing stories to tell! Each more terrifying than the other. So, I thought why not write a book together with them? The thought of making this book with these wonderful souls really pushed me forward, and I was immediately ready to compile their stories and write my own stories as well. The very next day, I had my laptop open and was typing up a storm.

The wonderful ladies provided me with their amazing and horrifying experiences, and I did the rest. My stories are printed towards the end of the book too, and I have given each of the authors their own little space to tell their story or stories in the book. I wanted to highlight each of the author's name and area of their story, and was able to do that successfully. And the table of content will show that effort successfully too.

I wanted to thank all these lovely ladies for sharing their fantastic stories to be read by the world and for all their effort in penning down their tales. These are just regular women, like you and me, living their quiet lives but still looking for their own small shining moment. Hopefully, this book will help us all grasp that moment and relish this small moment of success and happiness.

Contents

Introduction	1
Story by: Geet Bhambra	2
Your Wish is my Command	3
Stories by: Samina Namoji	8
The Predestined Destination	9
The Fateful Knock	13
Storie by: Syeda Aumme Salma	20
NEW DULHAN	21
THE SHADOW	23
My Handsome Grandfather	25
Permission Granted	27
Story by: Shaheen Razack	30
An Invisible Protector	31
Story by: Amrin Siddique	34
Lured to the River	35
Story by: Aisha Sultana	38
A House of Secrets	39
Stories by: Saba M.Bashir	46
Darker Than Dark	47
A Night Full of Terror	49
STRANGE RANTS IN JEDDAH:	51
Creature from Solitude	54
Story by: Aatqa Ali	56

He Was Never the Same	57
Stories by: Ashrafunnisa S. Zameer	60
Story 1:	61
Story 2:	63
Story by: Rashida Aliasgar Darukhanawala	65
A Call for Salah	66
Story by: Adeela Mushtaq	68
A Lone Lady	69
Stories by: Madiha Khan	70
Stories from USA	70
A Night in Michigan	71
Maha's Beautiful Room	75
A Story of Ohio	77
The Mimic	79
The COVID Horror	82
Stories From UAE	84
Sleep Paralysis	85
Friend or Foe?	87
Let's Live Together #1	89
Let's Live Together #2	91
Let's Live Together #3	94
Let's Live Together #4	96
Let's Live Together #5	98
Let's Live Together #6	101

Let's Live Together #7	103
Let's Live Together #8	104
Stories from Saudi Arabia	108
The Shared Hotel Room	109
Stories from Pakistan	112
A Consistent Entity	113
A Consistent Entity	116
A Consistent Entity	118
About the Author	*125*

Introduction

It is best to put this book down right now if you are a non-believer in all things paranormal or unexplainable! This is definitely not the book for you. Please just put it down and go pick up another "believable" or more "realistic" book, as you would say. Because this book is truly only filled with stories that will play with your sweet little rational mind. The stories within are so terrifying that it will be impossible for a non-believer to grasp.

But!

If you believe in the other realm, the Jins, the Churails, and the unseen, then this is the place for you. The collection of stories within is so scary that you might have to sleep with the light on tonight. After reading this, you will question every creak and crack of your home, every random sound you hear will sound ominous. But that's OK, because people like us thrive on this type of adrenaline. The rush that we get after terrifying ourselves is what we live for! And retelling these tales is our favourite pastime.

So, grab a cup of coffee or tea, dim down the lights, and immerse yourself in the world of the unseen!

Story By:
Geet Bhambra

Your Wish is my Command

The year was 1999.

Location: then known as the Tourist Club Area, Old Mazda Road, Abu Dhabi, UAE.

The loud thunderclap and lightning awoke me in a panic. It was early in the morning, and it was pouring outside, which is a pretty unusual thing in the UAE. Another unusual thing was that I was overwhelmed with the same eerie feeling I had felt 23 years ago. This feeling sent a chill down my spine. Trying my best to brush off all the doubts in my head, I turned and tried to sleep, but the whole reel played back in my head with all the minute details.

It was the beginning of the year 1999, and we had lived in the same building for over two decades. It was time for us to finally move out. Mom and Dad had already finalized an apartment, and it was just a few days before the move that they planned to show it to us and had started to get the maintenance work done.

The apartment was in an oblong off-white building and was very well integrated into the complex. It stood tall on a yellow tiled platform. The glass doors screeched as we opened them, stepping onto the white marble floors. We saw a distant staircase that went all the way up. Then there were two lifts with copper-coloured doors and a see-through niche. It was a very well-lit and welcoming entrance.

My parents had selected apartment #303 on the 3rd floor, which had 2 spacious bedrooms and a tiny balcony embossed in the building structure. Upon entering the apartment, I saw a huge, spacious lounge, and at the opposite end of the lounge was a dining area. I looked around and noticed broken tiles in the hallway, and I felt a heavy feeling, like something wasn't right. The maintenance team was already doing their thing, and my siblings and I moved to see our bedrooms. The bedrooms were down the hallway on the left as soon as you entered the apartment; the layout of the hallway was L-shaped. I opened the built-in wardrobes and found belongings of the previous owner left behind, like someone had just left in a hurry. There were some cloth hangers, a few clothes, a blue shirt, an iron box, and some wires. I remember telling my mom this, but it wasn't completely unusual. In our excitement about the move, we completely dismissed our doubts. Slowly, everything fell into place; the furniture, the TV connection, and yes, at that time, our new internet connection too.

Days and months passed by, and then came summer vacation. We did not travel that year, and our kids were the happiest. We had late mornings, had brunches, read magazines and comics, listened to the radio, played video games, board games, and decorated our room like the 90s teens. Weekends meant watching family movies, and my sister and I would go to the video library across the street to get the latest CDs.

One such weekend, my sister and I were crossing the road to our building when we saw a tall boy calling out my name and waving on the other side of the road. A little shocked and failing to recognize him, I ignored him and went straight to my house to tell my mom about this. The next day, that boy's mom rang my mom, and they turned out to be old friends. They became regulars in our house, and us kids would sit and talk about anything and everything.

On one such day, we started talking about the supernatural and their stories. I was 14 years old then and was beaming with excitement! I was so excited that I blurted out, "I wish I could see them, feel them, and their world." These exact words changed my life forever. We had dinner, said our goodbyes, and went off to bed.

Our room was set up with a double bed in the middle, a wardrobe on the side, and the bed also faced the built-in wardrobe. There was also a balcony with sliding glass doors on that side, and a bunk bed was right next to it. I slept on top of the bunk bed, and that night, I fell asleep with headphones still plugged in my ears while listening to the radio. I still remember the song I was listening to that night. At around 2-3 am, all of a sudden, I became conscious of my surroundings. The room was cold, and I

could hear the AC making its usual sound. I noticed a black shadow near the door, and within seconds, it had disappeared into thin air. I was able to see it clearly because of the reflecting street lights from the balcony, but then I shook my head in disbelief and went back to sleep.

In the coming days, I was awake most of the nights because our bed would start shaking all of a sudden. It felt like a minor earthquake, and in fear, I would hug my pillow tight. I started getting into deeper conversations with that boy about ghosts and spirits, and he made me believe even more in what I was experiencing. Our dolls started moving, their expressions would change, their eyes would shine brightly, and the cupboard doors would open and shut on their own, making all horrors come alive. Sometimes, according to my sister, I would sit for hours doing nothing, and one day I started speaking in a demonic voice. One day, one of my sisters was choked by someone unseen. We prayed, but nothing seemed to work, and my dad would blame the movies we watched and brushed off anything in disbelief because he did not see them first-hand. Financially and health-wise, things got worse.

Upon discussing all these happenings with this boy and his mom, we discovered they knew someone who claimed that they could save us from all this. In dire need to get rid of these events, we decided to go see him. But that was a mistake; it got worse. It got to an extent where I would be lying flat on the floor, and my face would be violently turning left and right, as if I was being continuously slapped. I felt like the demon actually lived as a parasite off me. I would scratch my arms with my fingernails, and that felt good.

My mom slowly started distancing us and herself away from that lady and her son, thinking all this was happening to us because of them. But the fact was, someone had actually abandoned this apartment because it was haunted, and we had moved into it. And I had openly invited them to show themselves to me in my excitement at this topic. And now that things were uncontrollable, mom and dad decided to just get out of this house, and we abandoned the house in the same way in just four days,

with a few of our belongings left behind, like the previous owner in a hurry. We were not even allowed to come back and check if we missed packing something. It was just, "Pack your bags and let's go!" My mom's words were, "Do not look back!"

This time we moved into a smaller apartment, and we were happy. Things got better, and we did well in our studies, and I even got a good job after a few years. One of my colleagues, Jaya, was searching for an apartment in the newspaper and through agents. She ended up looking in the same old building where we had stayed. This happened after many years of our escape. Jaya had an eerie feeling as soon as she got in the lift. She still looked at a few apartments in that building and loved it. While discussing more about rent and maintenance with the guard, he mentioned that the 3rd floor is sealed due to a supernatural presence (Jaya laughed it off, denying that and how she left in that lift). In apartment 303, people could be heard laughing and growling at night, and sometimes the lifts could go to that floor by itself, and no one would have pressed the button to call it there. People would even get stuck in lifts for hours. All the tenants of the 3rd floor had left the building due to this, and the owner had to seal the entire floor.

The next morning, she had a very casual talk with me regarding seeing an apartment in this building, and the guard detailed the happenings. I stood frozen with goosebumps all over my body, hearing her talk. I had tears flowing down my face as I told her about our stay in Apt 303 in that same building. I literally begged her not to rent any apartment in that building. Jaya looked shocked because I mentioned the same thing as the guard, and she then knew that the guard wasn't making up stories.

The news spread among the other tenants too, and later the whole building was empty for years until the owner decided to demolish it. Whenever I recall the incidents that happened in that house, I feel like I am transported to that year in that house. Now I really wish I shouldn't see them, nor feel them, nor connect in any way to their world. They don't leave you alone once they connect, but what makes you stronger is your faith. I still feel the presence of different beings in different places.

There is a new building in that very exact place, all pristine blue glass covered, but the question remains, is it still haunted? Or do they await another person wishing to show their presence?"

Stories By:
Samina Namoji

The Predestined Destination

The circular huts with thatched roofs seemed to beckon to them as the bus moved closer and closer towards its destination. After much thought, Gopal and Ravi had chosen this particular village for their thesis. As the bus came to a screeching halt, both young men took their baggage and climbed down. In this part of the rugged terrain, it was rather difficult to spot a village until you actually stepped onto one.

"Namaste sir! I am Mukesh, your local guide," said a deep-throated voice from behind them. Both of them turned to look at a young man, standing with hands folded in a blue checkered shirt and scruffy jeans. When he beamed a smile at them, his paan-stained teeth peeked out from behind his bushy moustache. "Namaste! It's nice to meet you," said Gopal and Ravi together.

The trio then proceeded to the place which was to be their home for the night. It was a clay and dung hut with a thatched roof. This was one of 'the most luxurious and popularly rented' out rooms. After stashing their luggage in the small hut, both friends surveyed their surroundings. The landscape was an arid, vast, and harsh desert that was punctuated by an odd tree or shrub. It was just eight in the morning, and already the heat was stifling.

With the hot wind gusting on their faces, Gopal and Ravi quickly chalked out a plan for their stay. They only had twenty-four hours before they moved on to their next destination.

Ravi spoke to Mukesh and told him all about the plan. "First, we need to tour the village, then go to the desert before sunset, and lastly, we will go to the Barah Fort," said Ravi. As soon as Mukesh heard this, his face fell. He said, "Sir ji, no one goes to the Fort after it's dark. It is not only risky, but also life-threatening. People say the fort is haunted." Listening to this, both friends burst out laughing and said, "Mukesh, don't you know there is no such thing as a ghost. Anyways, let's get moving on now. We don't have much time." Saying so, they proceeded to a camel cart. "Sir ji, this is the only means of transportation you will find in this village," said Mukesh, pointing to the camel cart. After stopping for a simple but rustic breakfast of methi bajra puri and aloo sabzi, they set out towards the village.

As Ravi and Gopal set up their camera and microphone, Mukesh was busy trying to convince the locals for an interview. A swarm of inquisitive children gathered around the trio as they adjusted the camera settings for better light. After wrapping up with the interviews and discussions, both friends observed that the villagers here led a very humble and modest lifestyle. Perhaps, nothing has changed over the course of several generations. Though both of them didn't fully understand the nuances of village life, it was still apparent to them that it was a tough life.

The camel cart moved sluggishly, trudging along the sands. Gopal wished for the cart to move a bit more swiftly in the suffocating heat. As they approached the desert, the bloody sky bathing the golden sun had begun to mellow down. Yet again, they hurriedly set up the camera for copious pictures of the desert in the dusk. Just then, unexpectedly, they were treated to a stunning myriad of performers, dancing and singing in the radiance of the twilight. As the men crooned, the ladies twirled around in a kaleidoscope of colourful Ghagharas (skirts). The diminishing light fell onto the mirrorwork of the Ghaghara, casting an ineffable glow, and the melody of the sarangi sliced the silence of the desert.

As if entranced, Gopal shifted the camera towards them. While he was busy capturing the performing artists, his eyes shifted to a blood-red silhouette. A lambani (peddler), wearing a brilliant red, heavily embroidered attire stood near a caravan of camels. Her dress was adorned with a maze of colourful thread embroidery, chains, buttons, and beads. As her wrinkled, dark kohl-rimmed eyes locked with Gopal's, he was drawn towards her. As she moved, her veil fell behind her, showing off her heavily tattooed arms and neck. Mukesh and Ravi followed Gopal towards the lambani (Peddler). She gestured her hands towards Mukesh. As soon as he got there, she looked at both the young men with her piercing eyes and whispered something in Mukesh's ears. While she was speaking, Mukesh seemed to freeze with terror. He turned around and, looking at both the friends, he said in a shaky voice,

"Sir ji, this old lady is saying that today is not an auspicious day for both of you. Some misfortune is going to befall you, and your lives are in danger. She has asked you both to return to where you came from."

A streak of anger flashed across Ravi's sharply chiselled face, and he said in a booming voice, "Mukesh, what is this nonsense? Is this a part of your trip? Sorry to say, but we don't believe in this baloney, and we shall be leaving right now." All Mukesh could do was shake his head. Then, he meekly went and sat in the camel cart, ready to drive it away. Both the friends hurriedly packed up their equipment and sat in the camel cart. The old lambani's eyes now watched both of them helplessly. They started to move ahead, but Ravi's head was clouded with the haunting words of the lambani.

As they approached the Fort, the last rays of the sun had seamlessly blended into the dark night. Mukesh was reluctant to accompany them, so they asked him to pick them up after an hour at the same place. As he left, they turned around to get a good look at the 'so-called-haunted fort.' The crumbling old fort stood eerily bathed in the pale moonlight. The haunted stories about the fort changed with each telling. Walking with bold strides, both of them reached a ginormous, frayed old wooden door. They pushed the rusty handle and went inside. A dank and musty smell hung about in the air. Old depleted walls that had stood the test of time appeared to be looking back at them. As Gopal shone his torch, Ravi managed to set up the tripod. With a minimal amount of light, they began to record and click pictures of the fort. The once colourful wall murals that told stories of a bygone era have now faded into oblivion.

Both of them were busy taking pictures; it was Ravi who first noticed a sudden drop in the temperature. "Gopal, are you suddenly feeling cold?" asked Ravi. By now, Gopal too had started to feel the frigid air surrounding them. He quickly felt a surge of unknown fear and dread. As he opened his mouth to speak, he saw something shadowy slide along the walls! Now, too scared to speak, he just pointed towards the wall. The shadowy figure had now begun to approach them rapidly. Just as Ravi turned around to see what Gopal was pointing at, the entity made a sudden lurch at them.

Both of them fell to the floor, not knowing what had hit them so violently. Grasping for breath, Gopal tried to strain his eyes and look around. Just then, he saw Ravi lying on the floor. He was frantically trying to push away something that was towering above him. Even though Gopal tried to help him up, they were both rooted to the ground. Now, the entity made a dash for Gopal. A thin black mist engulfed him, choking him so badly that he thought his bones would snap. As he tried to breathe, a foul smell filled his nostrils, making him want to puke. He tried with all his might to remember some chants that could help him defeat this monster, but his mind was numb with fear. As the grip tightened, his eyes bulged from their sockets, making them almost pop out. Then, he felt a twang of pain on his back, as if someone had slit his back with a sharp blade. He was screaming loudly, crying for help, but no sound came from his mouth.

Within a few minutes, the room started spinning around him, and he blacked out. After what seemed like ages, he felt someone shaking him vigorously. "Gopal, get up! Can you hear me?" said Ravi. Sitting up slowly, he could make out Ravi's face in the dark. "Are you alright?" he asked. "Yes, I'm okay," said Gopal. "Let's leave this dreaded place immediately," said Ravi. Staggering to his feet, Gopal tried to walk. "We'll come back for our things tomorrow. For now, let's get the hell out of here," said Ravi. Walking frailly, both of them stepped outside. In the dead of the night, not a soul stirred. Everything around them was at a standstill. Gopal walked slowly behind Ravi, still shaky from the experience. "We should have just listened to Mukesh and that lambani. It was very foolish of us to have come here and put our lives in danger," said Gopal. Ravi just nodded and walked ahead, not uttering a single word. "But all's well now. Thankfully, we'll be out of here by tomorrow," said Gopal. "Are you even listening to me, Ravi?" exclaimed Gopal nervously. Just then, in the beaming moonlight, Gopal's eyes fixated on his own shadow, falling on the walls of the old fort. He stood panic-stricken with horror, as he realized that only his shadow was present on the wall!

Now Ravi too stopped and gradually turned around, and slowly lifted his bowed head. A shrill scream escaped Gopal's lips, as he saw that Ravi's eyes were nothing but hollowed-out burning embers. As Ravi moved rapidly towards Gopal, Gopal tried to run, but his legs had turned to lead out of fear. As Ravi's hands clasped around Gopal's throat, a loud shriek echoed in the sky, and then it went dead quiet.

The Fateful Knock

(This story is based on true events).

As the last rays of sunshine melted away, and the darkness of the evening began to sneak in, Nilofar adjusted her dupatta (scarf) on her head and went up to the terrace to collect the dried clothes. The azan for the evening prayer could be heard loud and clear. She stood there for some time, mesmerized by the sound, but quickly gathered her thoughts as her little daughter Arafa started calling out to her. "Ammi!!!! Where are you???". "I'm here, my love," she replied with eyes full of love that only a mother could have.

Nilofar was the heart and soul of the whole neighbourhood. She was friendly, amiable, and had a positive regard for everyone. She always looked out for others, had a smile that could light up a room, and both the old and young equally loved her. But a few others had a different opinion. "A nosey Nancy is what she is, Miss Goody two shoes," said another. Still, these adverse thoughts didn't deter Nilofar from her goodness.

One evening there was a loud knock on the door. Arafa darted to open the door, only to find no one there. "Who is it, my love?" said Nilofar. "There's no one here, Ammi," said Arafa. As Nilofar tried to glance out, she saw what looked like a parcel near the door. She took it in and placed it on the table. She gingerly opened it, and what she saw made her eyes twinkle. "Oh, puris and kheer!" said Arafa, jumping up and down. This dish was a family favourite. "Yes, my love, today both of us will feast on it," said Nilofar, giggling. Night came, the table was set, and everyone sat down to eat. "Puris and kheer for me!" said little Arafa. "Who sent this???" asked Nilofar's husband, Javed. "It was left by our door this evening, but when I checked, nobody was there. It must have been Shagufta aunty. She knows how much I enjoy eating this," said Nilofar. The family then enjoyed their dinner and eventually settled down for the night.

In the middle of the night, Nilofar woke up with excruciating pain in her stomach. She clenched her stomach and woke Javed up. "What is it, my dear?" he asked. "Javed, my stomach hurts. I feel like someone's jabbing my stomach with sharp needles." As it was really late in the night, all Javed could do was give her some painkillers. "Have these, Nilofar, you will feel better," he said. Hoping for some relief, she quickly swallowed the tablet and tried to sleep. But with the shooting pain, sleep was difficult to come by. In the morning, Javed hurriedly took Nilofar to the doctor. After a quick examination, the doctor gave her some medicine to ease her pain. The medication seemed to have a comforting effect on her pain, and she thought all was fine.

But this euphoria lasted only for a few days, and on the fifth day, the stomach ache returned with a vengeance. Nilofar could neither move nor stand. Everything she tried to eat or drink made her vomit. This continued for a few days; she then began to lose weight rapidly and eventually became bedridden. Javed and little Arafa were inconsolable. The once chirpy, happy-go-lucky little girl turned into a mournful statue. All she asked was "Abbu, when will Ammi get better? I miss her very much." Listening to this made him feel more despondent, as there wasn't much, he could do to comfort either Arafa or Nilofar. Javed doted on his wife and left no stone unturned in finding her the best treatments. She was taken to every kind of doctor: general physician, ayurvedic doctor, hakims, healers, etc., but to no avail. All her reports and scans were normal, so there wasn't much any doctor could do.

By now, the pain had taken a turn for the worse. Her stomach ache started increasing with every passing minute, and she now needed to be given sedatives to calm down. Days turned into months, and slowly everyone around her started giving up hope, as her health further deteriorated. Nilofar had now become a shadow of her former self. Her whole body had turned into a pale, unbaked dough, white like a skeleton. Her eyes jutted from her sockets, and she stared vacantly at the ceiling. Her once infectious smile had vanished and had now given way to lips that were cracked and had become blue-black. She neither moved nor spoke; it was as if she had turned to stone. Suspecting Nilofar didn't have much time, Javed informed her family members about her condition.

Immediately, Nilofar's sister came over to see her, and after looking at her condition, she told Javed, "Javed, I suspect that Nilofar has been a victim of black magic, and I feel that a doctor will not be able to cure her. So, if you give me permission, I will call a Peer Saab from my city." Javed considered all this to be some old folklore, and his mind couldn't wrap around the fact that someone could harm his beloved wife. But since there wasn't any other remedy, and all he desired was for Nilofar's health to be restored, he reluctantly said yes.

So, the Peer Sahab was called upon. He arrived promptly and was immediately taken to Nilofar's room, who now lay in bed, almost giving up on her life. The Peer Sahab sat next to her, closed his tiny eyes, and gently put his warm comforting hand on Nilofar's head. He recited a few holy verses and blew all over Nilofar's body. Getting up, he then said, "I need a room for myself, and I will also need three big urns." This surprised everyone around, but nobody protested about it and did as was told.

The Peer Sahab asked for the urns to be placed in the room, and then he said, "Fill them up with fresh curd." This made everyone wonder what was up his sleeve. The urns were then filled with fresh curd, and their mouths were enclosed with a cloth, and tied securely. For the next 2 weeks, he sat in the room, and recited chants and holy verses. After those 2 weeks, he came out of the room and said, "I need a good strong rope." By now, everyone in the house thought that Peer Sahab was a lunatic, and he was just squandering precious time. But Nilofar's sister assured everyone that he had a very inimitable way of solving problems. So, they meekly adhered to his instructions.

The Peer Sahab took the rope into his old wrinkled hands and made a strong noose of the rope. He turned around and told everyone, "In sha Allah, Nilofar will soon make a speedy recovery." His words made both Javed and Arafa's eyes light up again. Finally, Allah had sent a ray of hope to them all. The Peer Sahab then asked for Nilofar to be given a bath, and her hair tied up in a tight plait. After this, she was to be brought to the room. As Javed entered the room, cradling Nilofar by his side, a malodorous aroma of tainted curd had occupied the entire room. The putrid smell made him nauseous, but surprisingly it had no effect on Nilofar or the Peer Sahab.

The Peer Sahab then said, "Javed, please make Nilofar lie down on the mattress." And then, to Javed's shock, he asked Javed to tie up Nilofar's hands and feet with a cord. A stunned Javed did as he was told. What happened next was truly mind-baffling for everyone present in the room. The Peer Sahab quickly secured the strong noose around Nilofar's feet, and then proceeded to suspend her upside down from the ceiling. After doing so, the Peer Sahab started his recitation. The recital of chants and holy verses had a powerful impact on Nilofar. Firstly, she started groaning softly, and then let out blood-curdling screams. This made everyone in the house want to claw their ears off. "Javed, help me please, my stomach is going to explode. I can't bear this pain anymore," cried Nilofar. But this didn't deter the Peer Sahab. He went on with his recitations. The more loudly he recited, the louder she screamed. By now Nilofar's voice had turned hoarse from all the screaming, and she hung motionless from the ceiling. Javed's handsome face was tear-streaked, as he stood and watched helplessly.

Exactly half an hour after the ordeal, the Peer Sahab asked Javed to leave the room. Then, armed with a thick stick, he broke the big urns of rotting curd. As the stench wafted into the whole house, it made everyone present there want to vomit. It was exactly at that very moment when Nilofar actually began to vomit. Her eyes fluttered open, and she began moaning in a loud voice again. She then started to jerk her whole body with wild convulsions. Initially, she threw up something green and gooey. Then a moment later, arching her whole body into a stiff curve, she threw up a big ball of human hair and some undigested food. After doing this, she went limp, almost as if life had been sucked out of her. During this ordeal, the Peer Sahab's lips moved in constant recitation. By now Nilofar was exhausted from all the goings-on. With a very feeble voice, she asked for Javed to be called. The Peer Sahab then gestured to Javed. Javed came rushing into the room to see Nilofar. The Peer Sahab said, "Javed, please get Nilofar down, and make sure she has a bath. See to it that she is put to bed in a clean place. I will continue the rest of my recitation there." Javed followed all the instructions to a T.

Once Nilofar was bathed and put to bed, the Peer Sahab then finished his recitation. He told the stunned and shaken family members that someone had performed black magic on Nilofar. Clumps of human hair had been mixed in her food, and that's what caused her to fall sick. If she would have been left on her own, she would have perished. He also advised them never to eat or drink anything that has been handed out by a stranger, as one can't fathom their intentions.

As for Nilofar, she slowly but steadily made a full recovery, and thankfully, this chapter in her life became a hazy past."

Stories By:
Syeda Aumme Salma

NEW DULHAN

The city of Hyderabad, shrouded in the shadow of the Qutb Shahi dynasty's dark history, bears secrets that whisper through the winds of time. In the vicinity of Qutb Shahi, where modern developments have spawned numerous colonies teeming with countless souls, a sinister tale from two decades past lurks. Back then, this area was but a desolate expanse, home to only a handful of houses, one of which harboured a newlywed couple taking their first tentative steps into wedded bliss.

Initially, their lives unfolded as idyllic as any newlyweds' might, a brief respite of happiness amidst the mundane. Little did they know that their harmonious existence would be shattered when a malevolent tempest descended upon their lives.

One fateful evening, as the couple sipped their tea, blissfully unaware of the looming terror, something unseen watched them from the shadows. The wife, her senses attuned to the unnatural, detected an eerie coolness in the air as the evening transitioned into twilight. A chill crawled down her spine, a premonition she chose to dismiss, and she continued with her routine.

Yet, ominous signs multiplied. Soon, the husband observed his wife retreating into the confines of a locked room, remaining there for hours on end. This strange behaviour gnawed at him, prompting his deep-seated concerns to manifest.

Days turned into nights, and the husband could no longer bear the mystery. During their usual evening tea, he confronted her, his voice trembling with unease. When he inquired about her extended isolation, his wife, in a paralyzing silence, locked herself in the room once more. The husband's sense of foreboding intensified.

His resolve hardened as he decided to investigate. Gazing through the window, he witnessed a surreal sight. His wife stood before a mirror, clad in a full bridal ensemble, her laughter reverberating through the eerie silence. The husband, petrified and mystified, watched as she conversed with her own reflection, trapped in a haunting dance of obsession.

For the following two days, the husband bore witness to the same disconcerting ritual, each instance plunging him deeper into a nightmarish labyrinth of despair. Realization struck him like a bolt of lightning – they were not alone. The spirit of the RANI, the forsaken queen, now tormented their existence, a narcissistic specter trapped eternally in her bridal garb.

Seeking refuge and salvation, the husband approached the Imam Sahab of the nearby mosque, their last hope. The holy man's counsel was chilling: flee the accursed abode immediately, for their house had become a haven for the vengeful RANI, a victim of a sinister dynasty conspiracy, haunting the premises as a "New Dulhan," a bride never destined for her wedding night.

In the dead of night, the couple left the city behind, their former lives forever tainted by the spectre's malevolent grasp. Yet, the spirit of RANI endures, her ethereal presence still lingering in that accursed house. Since that ill-fated day, the dwelling has remained desolate, an ominous reminder of the queen's relentless reign in the afterlife, where no soul dares to tread.

THE SHADOW

In the heart of the city, where the shadows conspire and the echoes of malevolence linger, stood a Tamarind tree, its branches whispering tales of terror. Legend spoke of these trees as favoured haunts of the Jins, entities that revelled in tormenting those who dared to encroach upon their spectral realms.

One Tamarind tree, infamous and cloaked in eerie tales, cast its ominous presence in the city's midst. Despite the ominous rumours swirling around it, a bold village soul decided to defy superstitions and set up a tea stall beneath its haunted boughs. "Chotu ka Chai Stall" swiftly became renowned for its otherworldly brew, drawing in crowds that sought both the warmth of Chotu's tea and the chilling thrill of the supernatural.

As the night unfolded its inky curtain, groups of friends flocked to the haunted tree, revelling in the camaraderie forged over cups of Chotu's infamous tea. Laughter and tales filled the air until, one ominous night, the fabric of their reality unravelled. Amidst their mirth, the distant sobbing of a lady metamorphosed into maniacal laughter and eventually culminated in blood-curdling screams.

Initially dismissed as a nocturnal symphony, the friends decided to explore the macabre melody. Their journey led them to a looming, half-constructed building, where the voices seemed to converge. With every step, the spectral chorus intensified, surrounding them in an ethereal maelstrom. Oblivious to the world around them, they ascended to the third floor, only to discover a lone cat, maimed and forlorn, with one ear cruelly torn asunder.

As they scrutinized the wounded feline, an unsettling revelation pierced their collective terror—its shadow betrayed a spectral form, that of a woman! Panic seized the group, limbs entangled as they fled the unholy abode. The cat, a mere vessel for the vengeful spirit, had left an indelible mark on their souls.

Racing back to the tea stall, they shared their harrowing encounter with Chotu, who nonchalantly revealed the feline harboured within the very Tamarind tree that loomed over his stall. Terrified by the spectral revelation, the group of friends, forever scarred by the unearthly encounter, vowed never to return to "Chotu ka Chai Stall." The haunting whispers beneath the Tamarind tree, a sinister serenade, persisted, echoing through the city's darkest hours

My Handsome Grandfather

In the bygone era before the haunting partition of India and Pakistan, within the confines of a secluded village, my grandfather lived as a young man. A paragon of rugged charm, he possessed a towering stature, chiselled features, and eyes that held a luscious brown allure. One ominous night, he stirred from his slumber, compelled by an unseen force that whispered in the shadows. A delicate melody, akin to the delicate tinkle of a lady's anklet, caressed his ears, coaxing him to unravel the mysteries concealed within the veil of darkness.

Driven by an inexplicable allure, he traced the ethereal resonance to the outskirts of his abode. There, bathed in moonlight, materialized a beguiling figure—a woman of unearthly beauty. Ensnared by her enchantment, my grandfather succumbed to her allure, forging a connection that transcended the boundaries of the mortal realm. Their clandestine encounters burgeoned into whispered conversations, and an otherworldly love blossomed beneath the shroud of the night.

As destiny unfurled its cryptic plan, my great grandfather orchestrated a union for his son, unaware of the spectral romance that had woven its tendrils around him. Obliging to paternal wishes, my grandfather entered into wedlock, blissfully ignorant of the supernatural forces that awaited the sanctity of their union.

The malevolent saga began on the inaugural night of their union, where the marital bed became a stage for the first act of a macabre play. My grandmother, flung from the bed, recounted a forceful push that defied reason. Simultaneously, as the clock tolled the ominous hour of 1 am, the haunting melody of anklets reverberated through the air, summoning my grandfather into the clutches of the enigmatic lady.

A chilling pattern emerged—each night, my grandfather would heed the spectral call, leaving behind a perplexed and agitated grandmother. The once-harmonious household echoed with dissonance, her patience tested by his increasingly erratic behaviour. Compelled by a desire to unveil the truth, my grandmother surreptitiously followed my grandfather into the nocturnal abyss.

Beneath a shadow-laden tree, she witnessed an unsettling rendezvous. The enchanting lady, a shapeshifting Churail, led my grandfather to a tree with a sinister orifice. A small hole in the gnarled bark became a portal to the supernatural, a conduit between realms. The revelation struck my grandmother with a terror that transcended the mortal plane—her husband ensnared by a spectral paramour.

In a desperate bid to sever the unearthly ties that bound my grandfather, the village elders decreed a drastic solution—to purge the malevolent entity, they would set ablaze the accursed tree. The flames consumed the arboreal conduit, seemingly severing the ethereal connection. Yet, only my grandfather, haunted by the residual spectre of a supernatural infatuation, bore witness to the Herculean struggle to liberate his soul from the clutches of the Churail. For when a spectral being entwines its affections around a mortal heart, the echoes of their love linger, eternally haunting the recesses of the human spirit.

Permission Granted

After the joyous union of my cousin brother and his wife, their lives unfolded in bliss and tranquillity. However, the elusive embrace of parenthood remained elusive for six years, casting a shadow over their marital happiness. Desperate for a remedy, they sought the counsel of countless doctors and embarked on a relentless pursuit of fertility treatments, yet the elusive spark of life eluded them.

In the midst of a family visit to Hyderabad for another cousin's wedding, the weight of their childless plight prompted a visit to a trusted Unani doctor. The diagnosis sent shivers down their spines, as the doctor, after a cursory examination of her nerves, uttered cryptic words, "There is no treatment for her here! You have to take her to the Ruqyah Centre."

The urgency of the situation collided with the festive air of the family celebration, creating a dissonance between the merriment and the ominous undercurrent. The mehndi function, a tapestry of joy and laughter, unfolded while the impending ritual loomed in the shadows. The cousin's wife, adorned with the task of applying intricate mehndi designs on others, concealed her silent anxiety behind the artistry of her skilled hands.

As the celebration reached its crescendo, the ominous spectre of their childlessness haunted my cousin's thoughts. Seeking guidance from my aunt, they resolved to heed the advice of the Unani doctor and summon the services of the Ruqyah centre post the mehndi function.

The appointed hour arrived, and with the Ruqyah practitioner on the scene, an eerie premonition enveloped the atmosphere. Children were ushered out of the room, warned that what unfolded within would be too unsettling for innocent eyes. Yet, fuelled by a misplaced sense of bravado, I and another cousin positioned ourselves near a window, eager to witness the impending spiritual ordeal.

As the verses of Ruqyah echoed through the room, a sinister transformation seized my cousin's wife. Her voice morphed into an otherworldly cadence, a vessel for a malevolent force that demanded interrogation. The Ruqyah practitioner delved into the entity's origin, unearthing a harrowing tale of a spirit that had committed suicide in the very apartment where the newlywed bride resided.

In a chilling revelation, the ghostly entity disclosed its past as a beautician, entrapping the unsuspecting bride with a mere invitation to enter her room. With the culmination of the Ruqyah, the spectral occupant was expelled from my cousin's wife, leaving behind an eerie silence.

The following day, the once-possessed bride exhibited an inexplicable transformation—she claimed ignorance of the art of mehndi application, a skill she had wielded with mastery only a day prior. The family rejoiced in the apparent liberation from the supernatural clutches, grateful for the return of normalcy. Allah's will manifested in a triumphant resolution, blessing the once-childless couple with the gift of three children.

Yet, for the witnesses who beheld the spectral possession unfold before their eyes, the traumatic memory lingered. The brave facade crumbled, and one cousin, overwhelmed by the grotesque reality, succumbed to the haunting spectacle, fainting at the intersection of the supernatural and the mortal realm. The first-hand encounter with the paranormal left an indelible mark, forever etching the thin veil between the seen and the unseen in their consciousness.

Story By:
Shaheen Razack

An Invisible Protector

It is an undeniable truth that my dad and his brothers carry this knowledge with them to this very day. Our roots trace back to the enchanting village of Kalusta in Maharashtra, India, where tales of a benevolent Jinn have echoed through the corridors of my paternal grandparents' home.

Allow me to paint a picture of the house layout. Nestled in the foothills, our residence includes sleeping quarters on one side, followed by an open passage akin to a pathway. Adjacent to it stands the kitchen, accompanied by a shower/bath area. Lastly, there is a separate room, shrouded in mystery, where the presence of ladies is forbidden.

Since childhood, we were regaled with accounts of the benevolent Jinn inhabiting the forbidden room. Imbued with a sense of reverence, we were instilled with the understanding never to engage in actions that might offend or harm the Jinn. Adhering to a set of rules was imperative—ensuring the room remained illuminated before Maghrib, refraining from consuming beef or steak within the confines of the house, and those partaking in such meals elsewhere had to cleanse themselves in the kitchen bath area before re-entering. Failure to abide by these rules, it was warned, would unleash swarms of scorpions upon the house.

In a moment of curiosity, I seized an opportunity when my uncle was sweeping the room to sneak a peek inside. The room revealed itself—spacious, pristine, adorned with aged clay pots, yet seemingly ordinary. During extended absences from the house, my uncle would perform Khatm (prayer) on chocolates, leaving them on a plate within the mysterious room. Plates entered but never emerged, a testament to our unwavering adherence to the established rules in our grandparents' lifetime.

The tranquillity was disrupted after my grandmother's demise when my youngest uncle, unaware of the consequences, extinguished the light after Maghrib. The repercussions were swift and severe—my eldest aunt fell ill and became possessed. Despite seeking medical and spiritual intervention, her condition persisted, and no remedy proved effective. It wasn't until my father connected the dots that the cause was traced back to the switched-off lights. The decision was made to keep the light lit day and night, yet, to this day, my aunt has not fully recovered her health.

Several years later, my youngest uncle shocked us by deciding to purchase an apartment in town and vacate the house. Perplexed by his choice, as he was one deeply connected to the house, he kept the reason shrouded in mystery. Only later did he reveal that the Jinn had visited him in a dream, instructing him to leave. After consulting with a Maulvi, he deemed it prudent to heed the Jinn's counsel.

While residing in Ras al Khaimah, our visits to the house during the holidays never yielded any discernible presence. Cousins who lived in the house echoed the sentiment—they never felt anything amiss. The Jinn, a guardian spirit, remained benevolent, intervening only when provoked or harmed, safeguarding each family member within the hallowed walls of that ancestral home.

Story By:
Amrin Siddique

Lured to the River

This incident takes us back to the year 1950 when my great grandmother was a young, beautiful woman, happily married and raising her children in a rural town in the state of Andhra Pradesh. Scarcity of water has always been a matter of concern in all villages, and this village was no different. Women had to rise even before they heard the roosters' crow. This was a daily routine; all women would pick up their water pots and head to the nearest spot on the river channel that passed through the village.

It was the month of May when the weather was hot and humid. They all set up their beds and called it a night. It was not long into the night before they heard a loud BAM! My great grandmother woke up to the sound of the Adhan. She lay in bed wondering what it was that kept her asleep till that hour. Without wasting more time, she sprang out of her bed, rushed to get her pot, and left the house. As she walked past her lane, crossing the road connecting the numerous lanes, she looked around for the other woman who usually accompanied her during this time to fetch water for their homes. To her surprise, not a single soul came into view. Ignoring this, she rushed towards the stream, feeling the cool breeze all over her face.

As she headed forward, she noticed that the huge temple on the right side of the road was still closed, and no one was around it. This seemed quite unusual to her, as it was supposed to be open by this time of the day, getting ready to invite its worshippers. Now she stopped and stood rooted to her spot for a little while, completely befuddled. While these out-of-the-ordinary occurrences crossed her mind, her pondering thoughts were distracted by the sound of the water stream that was at a close distance, burbling over the rocks and branches. This eventually made her move forward towards the river channel.

After a walk of about a minute or less, she reached the river channel that was a few steps below the road she stood upon. She held her pot on her waist, gradually getting down the steps. Just as she reached the last step, she bent forward, smelling the musky current of water that ran past so smoothly. She tried to clear the water right in front by dipping her hand in the stream and gently moving it to and fro for a few seconds. She then lowered her earthen pot in and filled it up to the rim, placing it on the step. As she tried to pick up the pot, she felt something jump into it and splashing water all over her arms. She was taken aback by this but gathered all her courage and peeped in, expecting to see a frog or some kind of fish maybe. There was nothing but clear water filled in. She took a deep breath and convinced herself that she was not ready for any more unnerving experiences.

Holding the rim, she tried to pick up the pot, but it didn't move a bit. She tried again but in vain. By this time, she was convinced that something wasn't right. She was petrified and helpless. All she thought of was to get home right away, no matter what. She recited Āyat al-Kursī and tried one more time, and this time she was lucky; the pot moved. But, wait! What was this? The little earthen pot turned out to be ten times its usual weight. She gasped and struggled to balance it on her waist. Breathing heavily, sweat all over her forehead! She didn't want to think of anything or even look around. She felt cold air blowing around her. Continuing to recite the verses of Āyat al-Kursī, she climbed the steps to the road carrying the exceptionally heavy earthen pot. As she rushed towards her house, she felt the sense of fear growing more and more, her pulse pounding hard in her ears. She didn't stop reciting until she gradually felt the pot get lighter. A lot lighter, and now it weighed as if it did every day!

After a little while, she sighed in relief, but that was short-lived. All of a sudden, she felt someone walking behind her. Not only did she feel the steps following her, but she felt someone's feet banging into hers from behind! With every step she took, a foot barged into hers. This was all getting worse. She cried in horror, wishing she had not woken up that night. Yes, this was all going on throughout the dead of the night. She felt nothing but helpless. Never in a million years was she going to turn around to check on who or what was following her. She almost began jogging her way back with the unidentified feet still colliding in her heels. Soon she was running for her life! As she reached the temple standing tall by her left now, she didn't feel her feet anymore.

Not sure what was going on, she continued running. By this time, she had crossed almost all the other lanes that came on her way back home. Now she only had one villa to pass by before reaching the lane that led her to her house. This is when she stopped and mustered all her remaining courage to turn around to see what was behind her. She turned around and was shaken to the core; she had never seen such a sight before. She saw an extremely tall entity covered in a white robe walking back to the river. It was as tall as the temple which it stood next to. She could not utter a word as she felt a sense of heaviness all over her body that did not allow her to move. All she thought of was how she had managed to get this far unharmed by this entity. She ran past the lane, reached home, and collapsed on the floor.

When she regained consciousness, she felt her body burn with a high fever. As she described her encounter with the entity, her family cried in shock and thanked God that they got her back all safe and sound. It was her faith that gave her courage and protected her that day.

Story By:
Aisha Sultana

A House of Secrets

Our world is diametric, filled with both good and evil, small and large, and black or white. Our creator, too, has created all his creations in contrast with each other. If we believe that good exists, then we have to believe in the bad too. Similarly, if one believes in God, then he has to believe in the devil too.

I come from a family where we believe in God and ghosts (Jins). My father always taught me to be strong and never be petrified of them, because they are not stronger than us. Here I would like to share some incidents that took place at my aunt's house.

After my aunt got married, she started to hear some ghost stories about the house she lived in from her neighbours. The environment was new for her, and she was trying to imbibe herself in it. Now with each passing day, she became more and more curious to know the truth behind these rumoured ghost stories. She started questioning her husband and her mother-in-law, but they shrugged it off each time and dismissed it 'as just a rumour'.

Once when she came to stay with us for a few days, she told us about the ghost. We, being the first to know about this, were so curious and excited to hear the story. Later on, all of us, cousins, decided to play on the Ouija board and talk to this ghost.

According to this game, you can call any spirits, talk to them, question them, and they would respond to you through the board. So, we started the game and called some random spirit, and asked it what the name of the ghost was that was residing in my aunt's house. To our shock, it spelled out the name 'MADINA BI'. So now, we had the name of that ghost.

To make matters worse, we all started to make fun of it, as we believed it was just a silly joke that one of us was playing. We never took it seriously until the following incidents took place:"

Incident #1: The Tape Recorder…

Once, my cousins went to attend a wedding, and as it was late, they stayed back at my aunt's place. They had enjoyed the marriage ceremony thoroughly and were relaxing by listening to some music on the tape recorder. My aunt was busy preparing dinner, and my uncle was watching television in the living room. Suddenly, the power went off. My cousin sister asked her brother to switch off the tape recorder, as it could have voltage fluctuations and had resulted in the power outage. So, her brother got up and switched it off, but he didn't unplug it. They continued with their chatter when, unexpectedly, the music started to play on its own from the tape recorder. Initially, my cousins thought the power was back, but the very next moment they realized that the switch was off! They both raced out of the room screaming, calling my uncle's name. My uncle listened to both of them and said very calmly, "That's really impossible, but for your assurance, let's go and check it out." My aunt too followed them. When they reached the room, my uncle saw that the switch was off, but the wire was plugged in, and the music was playing by itself… that too, without any power supply! He hurriedly unplugged it, but the music continued playing! He then tried to press the buttons on the radio, but he couldn't press even one button. It seemed like they needed a lot of effort to be pressed down. He tried it for a while, and finally giving up, he just shut the door of that room and took my cousins and aunt to my relative's house nearby.

This occurrence jolted them all very gravely. They spent the whole night thinking whether it was true or just a nightmare.

Incident #2: Suffocation

This incident took place with another cousin of mine. She had gone to my aunt's house for a vacation and had a great time there. After sightseeing, everyone was really tired, so they decided to hit the bed early. After dinner, they chit-chatted for some time and then went off to sleep. In the middle of the night, my cousin woke up feeling like something heavy was placed on her chest, and she was unable to breathe. She tried her best to turn left and right, but in vain. She wanted to call my aunt, but she couldn't utter a word. It felt like someone was sitting on her chest and suffocating her. She thought this was her end, and she was going to die. But somehow, gathering all her courage, she started reciting some holy verses. Finally, she managed to push away the hefty thing. She bolted from her bed, and hysterically screaming, she called out to my aunt. Aunty consoled her by saying that it must have been some kind of sleep paralysis.

All this had no effect on my uncle whatsoever. He never accepted that the house was haunted, and they continued living there.

Incident #3: Chilled to the Bone....

Once, I visited my aunt's house with my elder sister. We all had a fantastic time with shopping, delicious food, and sightseeing. As we met after a very long time, we sat chatting late into the night until around 12:30 a.m. Then, we all went off to sleep. My sister was sleeping beside me. I was so dead tired that as soon as I hit the bed, I went into a deep slumber. I usually don't get dreams if I am very exhausted. But that night, I had an awful nightmare.

I dreamt that I was running in a deep dark forest, and some peculiar giant was running behind me, with his hands wide open, as if he wanted to catch me or hit me. As I kept running, the forest became deeper and deeper. I had lost my way and was getting breathless. Ultimately, the giant was successful in catching me, and he hit my back forcefully with his strong broad hands. As soon as he hit me, I yelled loudly and woke up from my slumber. My sister also woke up and inquired about what had happened to me. I was shivering and crying nonstop like a small baby. Meanwhile, all this chaos had brought my uncle and aunt into our room. I was still trembling in shock and pain, even after waking up from my sleep, as I could feel a burning sensation on my back. I narrated my dream to everyone present there, but no one believed me. My sister made me recite some Holy verses and asked me to sleep with my head on her lap. I was chilled to my bone. As morning came, we immediately went back home. The memory of this incident will stay with me forever.

Incident #4: The Presence....

My aunt had never experienced anything strange, even though those incidents took place in that very house. She was always busy with her young daughter and other household chores. One fine night, she was sleeping on her bed. The bed was covered with a mosquito net (to protect them from mosquito bites).

All of a sudden, she felt like someone was staring at her, standing by the bed. She quickly opened her eyes and saw a blurry image of someone standing in an erect posture. For a second, she thought it might be her sister-in-law, then she realized that she was not at home. This terrified her, and she quickly turned around and woke up my uncle. My uncle, too, felt the presence. So, he swiftly got up and switched on the light. But there was no one around. They both recited some holy verses but spent a sleepless night. After that night, a very worried and shocked uncle and aunty confronted this matter with the elders of their family.

Incident #5: Encounter with the Priest

The previous incident shook my aunt and uncle to the core. They discussed this matter with the elders of their family, and it was decided to call upon a priest and cleanse the house. So, my uncle decided to call one of the known priests and explained the matter to him. The priest said that he needed to see the house first, and he had to spend a night in that house. So, my uncle agreed to whatever he said.

The next day, the priest came with all his preparations and inspected every corner of the house. He then recited some Holy verses and blew them on the water. This was sprinkled throughout every corner of the house. Soon after sunset, he went alone to a room that was attached to the main hall. He was not to be disturbed while he carried out some rituals. The door was closed but not locked. Everyone prayed to God that everything should go smoothly. The priest started reciting some holy verses continuously for about an hour or so. After some time, he started meditating, and then again, he recited some holy verses. He continued this pattern for a very long time. After that, he called my uncle and said that he had finished his job and was going to continue after a while.

In the middle of the night, at around 1 a.m., my uncle heard a loud thud, like someone had fallen from a great height. Soon, the thudding sound was followed by the screams of the priest. He quickly ran to his room and saw that the priest was lying down on the bed, and his right hand was on his chest. The priest was cold, and he was shivering, like he had seen something very disturbing.

My uncle somehow managed to pick him up and brought him to the hall. He then called an ambulance and took the priest to the hospital. The doctor said that the priest had suffered a minor heart attack, but there was nothing to worry about. He would be fine. The priest was under observation for the next two days.

When my uncle asked him what had happened that night, the priest said that he was attacked by the entity that was living in that house. He advised my uncle to leave that house as soon as possible.

Incident #6: The Final Straw….

The haunted house in which my uncle and aunt were residing wasn't easy to sell off because it was already infamous due to ghostly rumours around it. My uncle felt helpless. The only way was to abandon that house and rent another one. But he was emotionally attached to the house, as he was born and brought up there. However, this particular incident changed his whole perception.

My aunt's daughter, who was the only child, was about three years old at that time. She used to play all by herself and talk as if someone was sitting in front of her. Whenever my aunt saw this, she assumed it was pretend play and completely normal. One fine day, my aunt was in the kitchen busy with her daily chores, and her daughter was playing in the hall. She started shrieking, "I won't give you this, I will not, leave it, please, leave it." And all of a sudden, she started wailing. Hearing her painful cry, my aunt ran to the hall. When she asked her daughter why she was crying, her daughter pointed in the opposite direction and said, "That uncle hit me, mama." My aunt got petrified, as she saw no one in front of her. She then observed her daughter's arm; there was a red mark of fingerprints, and her arm was swollen. She quickly understood everything, grabbed her daughter in her arms, and ran out of the house to her neighbour's place.

Her neighbour inquired about the situation and consoled her. My aunt then called my uncle and explained the whole situation. She refused to step into that house anymore.

My uncle hurried back from work and took his family to his sister's house. The next day, my uncle went back to the house, took some necessary belongings, and left. He tried his best to sell the house for a couple of years, but he couldn't. Finally, after six years, the house was sold.

Initially, it was very difficult for my uncle and aunt to overcome this experience, but with time things eventually healed. These experiences were scary, but they will be everlasting memories for them and for the rest of my family who encountered them.

Stories By:
Saba M.Bashir

Darker Than Dark

Many times, strange situations leave us with no answers. We become speechless. Strange happenings, especially the interference of the other world, occur in our lives. Do we only believe in what we can see, touch, or feel?

But what if something unusual happens, something unbelievable? And because of those unbelievable circumstances, I present you with one more story. Today, when I came back to my room after sending my elder child to school, my middle child was crying silently on the bed.

"Oh dear, what happened? Why are you crying?" I felt immense love for him and took him in my arms. His reply was surprising enough to touch my heart.

"I saw a black shadow under the door. Why did you go out, leaving me here all alone?" He sobbed silently.

"It was my shadow, as I was coming towards your room." I reassured him and tried to keep my calm. "I have to send your brother to school, that's why I have to leave you here. You are my brave boy."

I gave him a tight hug and started getting him ready for school. But that shadow story was stuck in my mind. I kept wondering, what if he had really seen and felt something? This thought was terrifying.

It reminded me of an incident that happened a few months back. I was sleeping with my children in their room, and I had a dream. In my dream, I had a strong feeling that someone was standing at the foot of my bed. That feeling was so strong that I actually woke up thinking there really was someone standing by our bed. I looked around the room to see if someone was there, but thankfully, there wasn't anyone. This incident terrified me a lot.

I kept thinking about the shadow my son saw throughout the day, but soon I convinced myself that maybe he was crying because I had left him alone in the room while he was sleeping. Whatever the reason, I had to carry on with the day's chores, so I stored this matter in the back of my mind and went about my work. Gradually, I forgot about it as the days went by.

One night, I told my children a story about Bumblebee and Optimus Prime, their favourite characters, and after story time, we all went to sleep. While sleeping, I felt something. Our bodies and senses become alert when we feel there is something suspicious or dangerous around us. As I looked around towards the other side of the room, I caught a glimpse of a dark shadow in the corner, but as soon as I realized what I was looking at, it was gone! Vanished within seconds! I felt my blood turning into ice!

"What was that?" I asked myself. "Was it the same shadow my son had seen!? Was it real, or were my eyes playing tricks on me!?

As the days went by, I continuously tried to wrap my mind around what had happened! I then increased my prayers before sleeping, and after that, I never saw or felt that thing again.

But who knows what and when something is waiting for you…

A Night Full of Terror

I have always had a peaceful sleep ever since I can remember, and I could not have been happier! But once, I had such a strange night that has been locked in the depths of my memories forever.

This story is very close to my heart because it happened in my mother's home in Lahore. Many years ago, when I was 14 or 15 years old, we shifted into our new home. I was very excited about living in a new home—the fragrance of fresh paint, the brightness of the new floors, the ambiance—everything was a perfect dream for a teenager.

But our elder cousins started scaring us. They told us not to open the door without asking, as there were many robbers around our house, and they might come inside. My happiness was overshadowed by this scary gossip. As for me, humans are more dangerous than ghosts.

In a big family of 10, my grandfather used to sleep in the living room, and all of us kids had one bedroom to ourselves. One night, my grandfather had a high fever, and my cousin asked him to sleep in the bedroom with us as there was A.C in our bedroom, and my dearest grandfather was sick.

We were enjoying a movie together in our room, and we didn't know that outside there were roaring winds and thunder. We were so engrossed in the movie that we had no idea of the situation outside. After the movie ended, we got onto our mattresses to sleep.

Suddenly, all the lights went off with a loud thunder clap and winds that shook the house. As all this was happening, I noticed that someone had tried to open the door handle of our room. My heart was in my throat as I told my cousins around me; all of us were terrified. Someone was trying to come inside our house. I still remember the fear I felt as I was hiding on the other side of the bed. Then one of our elder cousins who was staying with us at that time picked up the receiver of the telephone to call our aunt who lived in the next lane. My cousin explained the situation, but my aunt didn't believe her. While she was on call with my aunt, the shaking and rattling of the room's door increased as if someone was trying to break down the door! My cousin, Aleena, put a heavy cushion beside the door, as if that would prevent the door from getting broken.

One of our telephones was outside in the living room. As Aleena tried to call the police, she realized that someone had picked up the telephone from the living room! We got even more terrified. It was confirmed that someone was in our home and was trying to get into our room. We were sure that robbers had entered our home. Somehow, we managed to call the police, and they called back to confirm our home number. As we were speaking to the police, someone again picked up the phone from outside.

Meanwhile, our door was about to get smashed due to heavy thudding from the opposite side. Fortunately, the police were already outside! But the story doesn't end here. It was still dark outside. The police asked loudly from outside if we could break the door or if we wanted to send someone from inside to open the door, as all the doors were locked!?! Everyone was shocked. How can this be? If there was someone inside the house, then how could all the main doors be locked? There were no answers and no time to think. My grandfather decided to go out and open the door.

We opened the door latch to our room slowly. "What if someone grabbed him? What if someone was waiting for us to open the door so that they could barge inside?" As these frightening thoughts were racing through our minds, we opened the door cautiously because we felt a little safe, knowing that the police were outside our home.

But thankfully, there was no one outside except darkness. My grandfather opened the lock of the main door without any problems. Police came inside and searched every corner of our home. Our aunt also came to check. Surprisingly, the police found nothing.

"Who was outside then? Who had picked up the phone!?" We were all shocked at this revelation! We kept wondering, but of course, there were no answers as there was no sign of a human in our home. Our bedroom door was damaged because of the heavy thudding. I don't remember when we all finally went to sleep, but that was the longest night of my life, and I can still recall every detail vividly.

On that night of terror, it rained so much in Lahore that it broke all previous records.

STRANGE RANTS IN JEDDAH

Have you ever plunged into the abyss of eerie occurrences, where the answers to your bewildering questions lingered in the shadows, forever elusive?

In the realm of advancing technology, we strive to unravel the mysteries, seeking the rationale and logic behind every phenomenon. Yet, the quest for a logical explanation is not always met with success; it often succumbs to the enigmatic forces that defy comprehension.

Now, journey back with me to the ominous year of 2015, a harrowing tale unfolding in the depths of my recollections. A frenzied urgency gripped us as we prepared to relocate to Jubail, Saudi Arabia. Our residence in Jeddah, perched on the 3rd floor of a foreboding building, bore witness to the trials that had befallen us. A tumultuous period marked by the loss of my husband's job, culminating in desperate prayers and arduous efforts that birthed another opportunity in Jubail, steering us toward an abrupt and unsettling movement.

In the dim-lit nights of Jeddah, I found solace in the eerie tales spun by my favourite paranormal program, "Who Kya Hay?" The echoes of spectral narratives reverberated within the confines of our dwelling, casting an unsettling ambiance, particularly when solitude embraced me.

One fateful morning, after bidding farewell to my husband bound for the office, I succumbed to an uneasy slumber, delving into a disconcerting dream. A sea of blackness enveloped me as an ancient phone rang incessantly, its eerie resonance resonating through the void. Amid the darkness, an intangible force seized my leg, a spectral grip that transcended the confines of mere sleep paralysis. In my struggle to break free, the ethereal malevolence yielded, releasing its hold as my eyes snapped open, my heart pounding in terror.

The tendrils of the supernatural extended their grasp to the soils of Pakistan. Nestled in my mother-in-law's room one night, I encountered another haunting dream. The feeble glow revealed me standing on the bed, tormented by a phantom assailant pinching at my right ribs. My screams, both in the dream and the tangible world, echoed through the silence, leaving an indelible imprint on my waking hours.

Returning to the sombre abode in Jeddah, a relic of unsettling occurrences awaited. An antiquated sofa, not of our choosing but a relic in our fully furnished flat, emitted disquieting creaks when occupied. One fateful night, as the nocturnal hours embraced us, a trip to the bathroom left my husband and me ensnared in a web of inexplicable terror. The sofa's unsettling groans heralded an unseen presence, followed by the ominous click of our room's door, a door that refused to yield to our desperate attempts. The room key, stationed outside, remained ensnared in an otherworldly clasp, leaving us bewildered and haunted by the mysteries concealed within the shadows. The events of that night persist as an enigma, etched into the fabric of our collective bewilderment, with the unsettling truth eluding us to this very day.

Creature from Solitude

We're all familiar with human prisoners, empathizing with those wrongfully confined behind bars. Their plight tugs at our hearts, and we yearn for justice to prevail. Yet, have you ever contemplated the inverse scenario? Can you conceive the existence of prisoners other than humans? Perhaps weak aliens ensnared by formidable humans, or animals and birds displaced from their homes?

Enter the realm of the supernatural, where Jins, poor creatures captured after dabbling in black magic, languish until their captors meet their demise or some miraculous intervention occurs. Have you ever spared a thought about these beings forced into committing malevolent acts against their own kind by nefarious men and women?

Let me unravel this mystery with the tale of Kumhari, a jinni (female entity) from ancient times dwelling in desolation, wielding the power to exact revenge and justice. Legends deem her the most formidable entity in the town, coveted by those hungry for power but formidable enough to resist easy capture.

This narrative unfolds from a real incident, witnessed on the program "Who Kya Hay," where human malevolence surpassed even the darkest forces. Kumhari, a spectral presence, casts a chilling shadow on those who dare utter her name.

In the desolate wilderness, a house stands abandoned, adorned with drawings of a girl with a red flower in her tightly woven hair. Empty rooms exude an air of desolation, harbouring an unseen presence that repels any attempts at prolonged stay. However, a man versed in dark arts, driven by greed for power, infiltrates the abode, seeking dominion over the Jins.

Under the full moon's glow, the man invokes dark forces, marking the moon and inscribing a circle on the veranda with owl's beak and feet symbols. Inside this protective barrier, he recites potent sermons, aiming to bind Kumhari to his will.

As the man loses himself in the incantations, he senses a presence, accompanied by the jingling of heavy anklets. Despite the protective circle, fear seeps in, unsettling the man's composure. An apparition materializes: Kumhari, adorned with a red flower, her paranda swaying.

Blinded by the belief that his spells have succeeded, the man steps out of the circle, only to be ensnared by the spectral entity. Kumhari, draped in black, drags him across the floor, silencing his screams and leaving behind an eerie stillness.

In this night of terrors, every plan is overturned, and the captor becomes the captive, swallowed by the ominous abyss of Kumhari's retaliation.

Story By:
Aatqa Ali

He Was Never the Same

Have you ever heard of an evil that can ruin your entire life? How just one interaction with someone can hypnotize you in a way that stays with you for a lifetime? I would never have believed in such nonsense until that one day when…

It was a scorching afternoon, and my mother was occupied with household chores. My siblings and I were engrossed in playing with our toys when we heard a loud banging on the main door. The abrupt noise startled us, and my mother, filled with curiosity, went to answer the door. It was our grandfather, looking frightened and sweating profusely. He urgently told us to leave everything and go with him to see my one and only uncle, who was in significant trouble.

Without much information about his condition, we hurried to see him. The moment I laid eyes on my uncle; worry consumed me. His clothes were torn, he breathed heavily, and his eyes were as red as blood—his devastated appearance sent chills down my spine. My grandfather explained that he found my uncle wandering the streets, attempting self-harm with a knife. As the adults ushered us into another room, a crowd formed around my uncle. Being a perceptive child, I sensed something sinister. My uncle seemed unconscious, resembling a scene from movies where a person gets possessed by an evil entity. The elders, in loud voices, deliberated on restraining him to prevent harm.

Locked in a room for hours, we anxiously speculated about the situation. Questions about who harmed my uncle and why he behaved strangely echoed in my mind. The uncertainty lingered until a sudden silence enveloped everything. Only the voice of an elderly spiritual scholar reciting holy verses punctuated the stillness.

In the ensuing days, my mother visited my uncle without divulging details. One evening, she finally disclosed that he was now fine. When we inquired further, she shared the unsettling encounter my uncle had with a strange man. The man, harbouring ill intentions, had adversely affected my uncle. Whether it was black magic or hypnosis, we remained uncertain. Despite improvement, my uncle was forever changed. The haunting memory impeded his progress in life. His job, marital life, and social activities were disrupted, and the fear persisted that the malevolent man might return. The incident had left an indelible mark, and my dear uncle now lived in perpetual fear, unable to escape the shadows of his own past. It's heart-wrenching to witness his struggles, but we all have our own monsters to contend with, and he has his own to face.

Stories By:
Ashrafunnisa S. Zameer

Story 1:

Back in the late '90s, we used to live in a very small studio flat. It had one big room, a partitioned area without any door for the kitchen, and there were two washrooms in the corner (it was railway quarters, and my father used to work in Bombay, India at that time, while we were living in Hyderabad, India with my seven siblings). Let me tell you that my mom is a very brave woman; she raised seven children all by herself because my father used to visit us twice a month or so.

We had newly shifted to this flat (I still remember the flat number C block-142), and in the beginning, for a few days, everything was normal. Then, slowly, my mother started noticing weird things. One night when we were all sleeping, we heard our mom shouting, "Who's there?!! Get off of there!!" She saw someone peeping from the ventilation window! As soon as she shouted, the people in the quarters surrounding us heard, and they came knocking on our door. They helped us search our apartment and ventilation windows, but they could not find anyone. We thought it might be some petty thief trying to find a way in and shrugged it off.

After a day or two, my mom got up to go to the washroom, at around 2-3 am. As she was walking to the bathroom, she heard weird crying sounds from the kitchen window. The kitchen window faced an open area in front of the building, so she thought maybe some animals were down there and dismissed the sound. When she was coming back from the bathroom, she noticed a woman sitting on the kitchen platform holding a bowl to her face. The bowl fully covered her face, only her blurry eyes were visible on the rim. She made eye contact with this woman, and poof she was gone. My mom got super scared and ran to her room, read all the duas that she knew. Soon, this became a norm; whenever my mom would get up at 2-3 am, she would notice a woman in a white saree with thick long black hair. She would read some duas, and she would disappear into thin air, then my mom would rush back to bed.

My mom then decided to inquire about the flat after a couple of nights of restless sleep. She asked around and got to know that there was a woman who hung herself in this flat before we had moved in. After this revelation, my mom called some religious scholars; they prayed and cleaned our place from anything negative. After that, we lived in that flat for seven more years without any incidents. But my mom learned a valuable lesson after this experience; from the next time onwards, my mother always inquired thoroughly before shifting to any new place.

Story 2:

In the year 2012, we moved to our own new house. The house was built on a big piece of land, so we used one half to build our home and kept the other half open. There was only one washroom back then, and it was built in an open space. It's essential to note that the opposite side of our house was also open land, with some trees and a fenced wall.

I had a habit of going to the washroom in the middle of the night. I used to go and keep the washroom door open. I tried to be brave and looked around every two seconds for anything suspicious. As days passed, I started to think I was very brave. I would continuously watch the distant trees and imagine what if something or someone came from there. Thoughts like, "Would I be able to escape? How would I escape? What would I do?" lingered in my mind. No matter what, I had to look at those trees. Even if the trees moved because of the wind, I would gather courage and keep looking. By watching the trees, I consoled myself, convincing myself that nothing was there and everything was normal.

One night, as I was watching the trees as usual, something unexpected happened! Suddenly, I saw a very tiny lady jump out of a tree! She jumped onto the fence! She had white hair and walked very fast on our fences, running towards the right side, to our neighbour's building. I was trying to understand what was happening, but I couldn't grasp the situation! As my brain started to comprehend, I was already running back inside our house, leaving all my bravery badges in the toilet.

The next day, I had a fever, but I could hear gossip around the house about how the neighbours had started noticing ghosts. Soon, all the neighbours began writing a slogan on their walls that said 'O Stree Kal Aana' in Hindi, which means, "O lady, come tomorrow." Next to this sentence, they would put a handprint of turmeric and red chili powder. This wasn't just happening in our colony; even neighbouring colonies did the same.

In fact, this incident was covered in many local newspapers (The Hindu). I couldn't believe I actually saw something and lived to tell the tale!

Story By:
Rashida Aliasgar Darukhanawala

A Call for Salah

In our hometown, our house was right beside a mosque. My grandmother used to tell us this story all the time because it was something she experienced herself.

When she lived in our hometown house, she witnessed strange happenings, especially around Fajr time. Strange noises would reach her ears, like someone waking up and going to the bathroom. She could hear running water from a tap in the bathroom. After the water sound stopped, it seemed like someone was walking around the house, visiting each family member's room. After a while, it felt like someone was trying to wake them all up for Salah.

Everyone was puzzled and had no idea what was happening. So, one day, they decided to ask the Moulvi Sahib of the mosque next door about these occurrencaes. The Moulvi Sahib listened intently to their query and, after smiling a little, told them that their house was next to a mosque, and there were pure jinn residing in their house. The jinn would never bother them but wanted them to offer Salah on time.

Even though the jinn didn't cause them any problems, it was still very scary to stay in that house. They eventually shifted to another place and never experienced anything like this again. Alhamdulillah!

Story By:
Adeela Mushtaq

A Lone Lady

This happened with my Dad back in 1999-2000, around 20 years ago. We used to live in Satwa, where the buildings were designed to resemble colonies, known as Satwa Sheikh Colony. Similar buildings are still present in Qusais. These structures had a large open ground in the middle where all the children used to play. There were three sides with flats, each side featuring an open staircase to the floors, allowing us to always see people going up or coming down.

My dad used to go to work really early every day, usually around dawn, just before sunrise. We lived on the ground floor. One day, while he was leaving, he noticed a lady sitting on the stairs with her head bowed down onto her lap. My dad thought maybe she was waiting for someone. At that time, some mothers used to wait with their kids for school buses, so my dad passed by her without looking back.

As he was heading out of the building towards his car, he heard someone calling out for him, but in a very low voice. He still didn't turn back as his name wasn't being called.

When he finally sat in his car, he saw the same lady passing through the walls of the building. He got really scared and mentioned that the lady's face wasn't visible because it was covered with a scarf. He started driving his car, and while moving, he could see the lady moving through the building walls at the same speed as him. After that, he drove off really fast, so scared that he didn't even look in his rear-view mirror and kept reading surahs. Since that day, he has avoided going out of the house during those early hours. He also told us never to look back when it was dark outside, because you never know who is waiting for your invitation.

Stories from USA

By: Madiha Khan

A Night in Michigan

This happened in Michigan a couple of years ago. Whenever we have a family reunion, we take a little family vacation together, exploring other states (most of the family is originally situated in Chicago). This time around, my sister Hina planned the trip so that we would explore Michigan and the islands around it. These islands were only reachable via a ferry and didn't have any cars or buses within the island itself. The residents of the islands used horse-drawn carriages, bicycle-drawn buggies, bicycles, etc., as their form of transportation around the islands.

Our trip was memorable! We had a fantastic time. It was a well-organized one-week trip with hotels that Hina had booked in advance for our overnight stays. Everything went super smoothly except for the last night...

After we had our island fun, we all got back on the ferry and headed back to the dock where our cars were parked. We were in two vehicles: the van driven by my dad (with my mom as a substitute for him for when he got tired), and the other vehicle was driven by my brother Nabeel (with Hina being his substitute).

It had gotten a bit late, and our reservation at that night's hotel had been cancelled. So, we all pulled out our phones trying to find the closest hotel with a family room or two king-sized rooms to accommodate 10 people. We started calling hotels within a 50-mile range, but since it was late and we were a group of 10 people, we were turned down. Just as we were getting a little disappointed, Nabeel hit the jackpot! There was a family room available at a hotel that was 30 minutes away!!

We gave a collective cheer because we were tired, hungry, and sleepy! My kids were dozing off as we entered the address on the GPS provided on the hotel's website.

As we entered the little (which is an understatement if I am being honest) minuscule town that the hotel was located in, we noticed how deserted it looked. Think of any of those movies where people just up and leave, and the streets, stores, etc., are deserted. No cars, no people, and even the one gas station they had was also closed! A wave of nervous laughter went around in both cars, but then we spotted a Taco Bell! Though we didn't expect it to be open (Hello! The gas station was closed!), we still pulled up to the ordering area through the drive-thru and were greeted by a chirpy girl, a huge contrast to the situation we saw around the town! Yes, we were shocked but relieved that there were actual humans there. We ordered and got our food and headed to the hotel.

We drove in circles looking for the hotel, but this town had like 5 streets! And we could not locate it! Till we saw a small road right next to the gas station... and there it was!

On the pitch-black street stood a huge, white marble building with an even bigger DESERTED parking lot.... guys, there were only 2 cars there....

We parked the car, got out, and kind of paused, wondering if it was even open. Then we joked a bit but still walked in. Maha (the youngest sister) carried my sleeping kid #1, while Nabeel carried sleeping kid #2. We all quickly grabbed whatever we thought we would need for the night and headed in. But as we entered the hotel, we completely forgot about the weird deserted town, with the weird lonely hotel with now 4 cars in its parking lot. The place was huge and beautiful. Except for the one person manning the desk, it was completely empty too. We didn't care; we got the key card to our room and went up. The 'room' or hotel apartment, as I would call it, was huge! It had 2 king-sized beds, a pull-out bed, and it led into another room with bunk beds and another king-sized bed! My parents took the room where the bunk beds were. Maha slept on the top bunk, and kids #1 on the bottom. In the other room, Hina and kids #2 slept on one king-sized bed, Nabeel on the pull-out bed, and my husband and I on the last bed.

As soon as we got there, we quickly ate our food. While we were eating, we started hearing voices outside of our room... of kids crying, which was, of course, normal because we were in a hotel. But soon we realized these sounds were coming from right outside our door. Then, all of a sudden, we heard some kids running in the hallway outside our room. Feeling brave all of a sudden (I don't know what took over me), I quickly went to see these 'kids.' I jerked the door open to find the long-deserted hallway; there was no one there!!! So, I was like okay. They have probably gone into their rooms. But the same thing continued well into the night. Who knows, maybe some kids were playing hide and seek (at 2 am), or that's what we made ourselves believe. Then, when everyone settled down, and snores started filling the rooms. I, obviously, am unlucky enough to always fall asleep last. Hate myself for it, but that's my life. Farhan (husband) dropped off to sleep within seconds, and on the other bed across from me, Hina was a goner. But I was relieved to see that Nabeel was up, as I could see his face light up by the light of his phone. He was across on the other side of the room, but then I heard knocking on the walls. It was a clear knocking sound, coming from my parent's room. My parents' bed was against the wall that I could hear the knocking from. The knocking continued for 5 minutes, when there was a lull in the knocking, I finally gathered up courage to whisper screamed to Nabeel across the room:

Me: Nabeel, did you hear that?

Nabeel: Yepppp.

Me: It's coming from Mom and Dad's room, right?

Nabeel: Yeppp, lemme check if they need something.

He gets up and checks.

Nabeel: Mado Appi (me), they are all asleep. So, I have no idea who knocked. And on that note, I am gonna sleep too. Goodnight.

Me: Noooo!!

I started praying all the prayers that I know! I read everything, EVERYTHING that I know and then turned on the lamp next to me. NO WAY was I going to sleep in the dark. The knocking stopped thankfully, and while I was reading the prayers, then thankfully I too drifted off. At around 3ish am, all of a sudden, I woke up. Only to see a huge dark shadow (8 ft tall?) standing next to me; it was bent over, looking down at me, as I slept on my back facing the ceiling. I squealed, shook my head, and blinked, and all of a sudden it was gone.

GUYS, NO ONE WOKE UP! What was wrong with them!?! I literally kicked my husband, but he didn't even stir!!! He was facing the other way. So, I ducked my head under the blanket, scooting all the way down off my pillow and literally hid my face in my husband's back and prayed till I fell asleep again. In the morning, my mom woke up Farhan.

Mom: Farhan, where is Madiha (me)?

Farhan (while trying to understand what was going on in his deep sleeping haze): Huh? She is sleeping.

Mom: WHERE?

By this time, I had heard her. I stuck my head out from under the blanket and said: I'm here. She laughed. She said she had been trying to find me. She looked in the bathrooms and even checked on the floors next to our beds to make sure I hadn't fallen off the bed. In the end, she had been so worried that she had woken Farhan up. She couldn't see me at all because I had made myself one with the bed and my husband. Oh, yes, I gave Farhan hell for sleeping through my hellish night. Maha (the younger sister) woke up with an unbearable pain in her arm, and it was so terrible she couldn't move it. She lay in her top bunk bed in the other room and was unable to move. Then my mom forced her to come into our room, and all of a sudden, her pain started subsiding. Hina, the kids, and I went exploring the hotel while everyone got ready to leave, and we found a huge lake at the back! It was beautiful but eerie; we did have our breakfast sitting by the lake, but it explained the pitch-black darkness.

Maha was completely fine as soon as we got out of that hotel. We left right after breakfast, but it was one hell of a night!!

Maha's Beautiful Room

My younger sister, Maha, has such a beautiful room. She has decorated it according to her personality, and it's like a little museum where you can discover things about Maha as you go through the room. But there is just one problem... her beautiful masterpiece of a room might be a teeny tiny bit haunted. Ok not teeny tiny but a little bit more than that.

Whenever we visit, I love staying in her room (Note: It was my room before I got married; when we had first moved into that house, I had called dibs). So, when I visit my mom's house, I would stay there, and yes, we would hear random rustling sounds at the foot of the bed, random knocking on the walls, and not from the walls that are connected to the other room but on the walls that have nothing on the other side. There are no trees near that room, and it is on the second floor, so there is no way anyone could knock on the walls.

But these are all just minor things and don't bother us and her that much. Nothing a little bit of Āyat al-Kursī and false reasoning can't solve.

Then two slightly bothersome things happened that made Maha stop and say: "OK Pause! Wow!"

First: Maha woke up one fine morning and heard Ammi calling her and Nabeel (younger brother) from downstairs for breakfast. So, she went down to have breakfast with Nabeel coming out of his room, and following right behind her. It was just Nabeel, Maha, and Ammi at home. After breakfast, Maha and Nabeel went upstairs to get ready for the day, only to find Maha's room a complete mess! Her bed covers and blankets had all been removed from the bed and were thrown on the floor. Her rolling chair had been flipped over, with blankets all around it too. Nabeel swore he didn't do it, but how could he, when he had gone downstairs right behind Maha.

So that was one of the scariest and undoubtedly real things that had happened to her.

Second: She was basically alone in the house for the weekend. Baba had gone to another state for some work, Hina (sister) was at her own house, Nabeel had gone with Baba, and Ammi had gone to perform Umrah. She, all of a sudden, lost her wallet. Looked everywhere. Bed, dressing table, under the bed, closet, downstairs, basically everywhere. She searched for it the whole weekend. All her IDs, credit card, and most importantly her license was in it. So, when at last she had given up hope of finding it (2 days later), she decided to first go to the DMV to get her license re-issued, then she was going to cancel all her cards. When she started to get ready to go out, she saw her wallet sitting right on the dressing table. I mean she checked this place multiple times! She tore her room apart looking for it, and she uses her dressing table a lot, but 2 days later, when she is about to take action about her missing wallet, it is just right there on the dressing table.

Now I know many of you will say it must have been there all along and she didn't see it. But seriously, who would take such drastic action if they really didn't search everywhere thoroughly?

It is basically a "believe it or not" situation. But I believe it because no matter how our brain tries to rationalize it, these things are out there and they are real.

Now it is up to you... believe it or not, it happened and it was a thing I couldn't wrap my mind around as overlooking.

Not when I, myself, have lived in that room, with all its creaking, rustling, and knocking. The cover thing was probably the most dramatic thing that had happened in her room, other than that it has never felt too threatening, Alhamdulillah.

Maha is fine with her room and loves it! If it was up to her, she would never leave it! Other than that, we live through things, we get surprised or scared, then we forget and move on. And Alhamdulillah for that!

The human brain is an amazing thing; it can overlook everything and rationalize it all and then forget it!

Truly, Allah is remarkable to make us this way. Subhan Allah

A Story of Ohio

A couple of years ago, we were all gathered at my younger uncle's house in Ohio. It is said that there might be something in his house. Even though whatever it is never bothers anyone, it is still there.

It was my cousin's white coat ceremony. He was receiving his white coat to start his studies at medical school. Most of my family who live in America wanted to be there to support him and cheer him on. So, Masha 'Allah, around 5 families, which were around 25 people, all drove or flew over to my Chacha's (uncle) house. My Chacha has a big house, and we all were easily accommodated.

But of course, once all the cousins are gathered in one spot, who has the time to sleep!? After dinner and some chit-chat, the adults decided to turn in. The cousins all sat in the downstairs area in the living room, which is also attached to the dining room, and the dining room is attached to the kitchen. We can see all three rooms if you are in any one of the rooms.

We all sat around talking, catching up, laughing, some making noodles or chai, others raiding the pantry for junk food. Basically, we all hunkered down for an all-nighter. And soon enough, it was 4 am. And as most late-night chatter goes, we were telling scary stories!

As we were still engulfed in our chatter and terror, all of a sudden, we heard someone coming down the stairs in the room next to us. We all froze, thinking one of the adults had come down to tell us off for being up too late (Yes, we were all adults there, but we still get scared when our elders catch us staying up too late into the night). By the way, the houses there are made of wood, and we can hear every creak and step anyone takes upstairs or downstairs.

Anyway, we all froze, waiting for someone to come. And then, all of a sudden, we heard the front door of the house open and slam shut! Now, there was pin-drop silence in the room we were sitting in! We all stared at each other wide-eyed! The same question on all of our minds:

Who is going outside at 4 am in the morning!? Because of the ghost stories, we were all at our wits' end. All of us were frozen to see if anyone would come back through the front door.

So, after five minutes of nothing happening and us just sitting there in silence, I looked at my younger brother, Nabeel, and whisper-screamed to him:

"Nabeel, go check who it was! You are the biggest."

Nabeel (trying to shrink his 6'2 frame into his sofa): "Why me!?! You are older than me! You check!"

Yes, we are both scaredy-cats.

Then our eldest cousin got up bravely and quickly went to check who it could have been. We heard him open the front door and heard him going outside. Then he came back in and said,

"Um, there is no one outside."

So, all of us stood up at once and said:

"Well, this was great! Time to sleep!"

And literally all the girls ran upstairs, and all the guys ran downstairs. (Guys were sleeping in the basement).

Ooo yes, we laughed about it later on. But at that time, we all freaked out!!! There is no doubt we heard all these sounds, and the fact all of us heard just makes it even more real. Whatever it was, probably wanted some peace and quiet and wanted us all to sleep.

The Mimic

My younger brother, Nabeel, is the sensible one in our family. He thinks logically and tries to solve all the problems instead of creating them. So, when he told me these two stories that happened to him, it really freaked me out.

Story #1

This one happened in my mom's house, which, if you have read the story before this one, you should know is haunted.

My mom and dad travel a lot; they go to different states for all the exhibitions my dad organizes. Sometimes Nabeel is home alone, and sometimes Maha is home alone, but they go to Hina's house at night to stay over. This was before Nabeel was married; now, mash Allah, he has his own house, and he lives there.

This story happened a couple of years back. So that day Nabeel was home alone, and he was taking a nap. He had woken up with the feeling of something heavy on him. He felt like there was a weighty thing on his chest, and started thinking:

"What is happening? Literally, no one is in the house, and even if there was someone in the house, no one was going to come and sit on my chest."

He tried to open his eyes, and before he could actually open his eyes, he heard a growl right next to his ear! This is when he freaks out! He told me that he literally heard a really guttural growl next to his ear, and he couldn't understand what was happening! He jumps off the bed, opens his eyes, breathing hard, and quickly looks around the room, but there was no one there. Nabeel tried to pass it off as a bad dream to calm himself at that moment, but he knew that something was not right. He told me later that he knows what he heard and he had no doubt that it was real, but at that moment when he had jumped up off the bed, he needed to tell himself that it was nothing but a dream; otherwise, he would have lost his mind.

Story #2

This one happened when I was visiting. We were all staying over at Hina's (younger sister) house. Ammi and Baba had another exhibition in another state, so they were traveling. When it was time to sleep, Nabeel decided to go home (Ammi's house). I tried to freak him out about going home alone and sleeping in an empty house. He said, 'Oh Appi, it's OK!' and then he went home.

After about an hour later, we got a call from him, asking us if we had forgotten something and had come home to get it. We, obviously, had not even moved from our spots on the sofa and said "no." Hina asked him if everything was OK. He said that he was in his room and he heard the main door of the house opening and closing, like someone had entered the house. Then he heard Maha (younger sister) say 'Bhaiya' (Big brother), he answered her calling out 'Yea', but there was no reply back.

After 5 more minutes, he heard it again 'Bhaiya!' This is when he decided that she couldn't hear him, so he got up from his room and went to the staircase that connects to the bottom of the house, and from there you can see downstairs and see if whoever is calling you from the bottom of the stairs. When he got there, he yelled out, 'Yea Maha! What do you want?' but there was no reply, and when he bent forward to peer downstairs, he saw that the bottom part of the stairs was in complete darkness.

Then he called out again. "Maha?" but obviously nothing. He quickly read Āyat al-Kursī and called us. He clearly thought we were pranking him, and I had tried to scare him before he left, had him doubting us even more.

Hina said, 'Nabeel, don't go downstairs! Just come to my house and sleep here!' He told her not to freak him out and that he would just lock his room and sleep there!! As if a locked room could keep anything paranormal out!!! We were shocked! He actually just slept there ALL ALONE! And that is why he is a weirdo!

These things have happened before in my mom's house, and we always dismiss them as a trick of the light or rationalize them somehow. We would see shadows in the corner of our eyes all the time. I would be sitting doing homework on the computer late at night after everyone had gone to sleep, and on my right side, there would be a doorway where I would see the stairs, and I would see a shadow going on the stairs from the corner of my eyes. And when I would turn my head to look, there would be no one there. So, I would go back to doing my homework. Alhamdulillah, we never heard voices or felt anything negative until recently, and that too only with Nabeel and Maha. But Alhamdulliah, my mom and dad have never felt anything, and to this day, they continue to live there happily, Masha 'Allah.

The COVID Horror

This story took place in the States. I had gotten sick after attending my brother's wedding (yes, I had gotten Covid), and so far, no one but I had tested positive. So, they had very 'nicely' thrown me out of the house. In other words, they had moved me to a very nice hotel and given me a credit card to eat to my heart's content and to have fun!

But obviously, Covid is no walk in the park. After the first 2 days, I got a high fever, stuffy nose, body ache, upset stomach, etc. The worst part was me being stuck in a room for 6 days all alone. My sister and cousin were in the room next to me, but they might as well have been at home because they weren't allowed to stay in the same room as me. They were there just in case I needed something to eat or if I got worse.

Anyway, on the 5th and last night before I was to be moved to my sister's house (who had also confirmed to be Covid positive along with her whole family), I had moved to another room because my original room's window had broken!

They had upgraded me to a suite because of the broken window. But as I walked to get to the suite, it turned out to be at the furthest corner of the hotel. Half of that area was closed up for renovations, and the rooms that were occupiable were vacant. I didn't pay much attention to that in my excitement because, wow, a suite all to myself! But as I stepped into the room, I realized that it had a gloomy feel, but I shrugged it off and kept up my excitement. Maha (my siingster) had actually fought for the room because they had put me in a broken window-room and no one had been able to fix it.

That night I felt uneasy. I felt lightheaded while getting ready for bed, which I associated with my sickness, and somehow managed to get ready for bed and pulled myself onto the bed. There I lay motionless, after turning the TV on. When I felt I couldn't keep my eyes open for even 1 sec, I put on Surah Rehman. I had been sleeping every night while listening to Surah Rehman (because it's supposed to help heal the sick quicker), and usually, I would fall asleep with the Quran on till

I woke up again and turned it off. This helped me sleep because I don't like sleeping alone. The Quran helped me relax and put my fears at ease. So, with the phone in my left hand, I drifted off to sleep. I slept in one position, my neck turned to my left side, looking at my phone while listening to the Surah. On my left side, I could see the entrance door, but I fell asleep almost immediately.

The next time I woke up, there was a black blur standing by the entrance door, the shape of it wasn't human.... it was.... it was like someone had covered themselves with a huge black bedsheet and was just standing by the door... (I had slept with ALL the lights on of the room because I was scared to sleep with the light off) After I saw this, I lifted my head to see it clearly, but it was gone! Then I realized there was silence in the room, which I found odd because my phone had been on when I had fallen asleep. As soon I realized that, I realized my phone wasn't even in my hand! It was on the other side of me, tossed to the other end of the bed!

For the past 5 nights, it had NEVER turned off by itself. It was on auto play and kept playing surah after surah. But this time, it was paused mid surah!!!! AND turned off! I shot up in bed! And read all the prayers for protection that I knew from the Quran and turned on the TV with the volume turned up! At some part of the night, I fell asleep again while watching TV, and this time when I opened my eyes, I was facing the right side of the room, and yeppp, I saw it again, standing in the shadows by the window.... it disappeared again. And as I sat up again terrified, I realized it was 7 am.

I got ready quickly, packed up my stuff in the room. And waited for Maha and Wardah to wake up (they were two floors above my room). By 9 am they hadn't woken up. I continuously called them till they woke up. At 10 am we checked out, and I breathed a sigh of relief. It was such a terrible experience. The fact that I was alone and was being targeted over and over was too much for me! I mean it had turned off my phone and it was tossed to the other side of the bed!! This was so physical and a clear indication of it not being good! It was way too much for me, and I was so glad to be out of there!

Stories From UAE

By: Madiha Khan

Sleep Paralysis

This story isn't necessarily scary, but for me, it was an extremely terrifying experience.

10 years ago, I got in an accident while jet-skiing, and yes, it is totally as painful as it sounds. By some miracle of Allah, I survived and with all my limbs intact. I did have many injuries, like some ruptured muscles on the left side of my back, a couple of bruised ribs, and one slightly chipped rib. Yes, I went through years of physiotherapy, doctors, and medication. Obviously, the painkillers and relaxants I took were extra strong because the pain was unbearable. These medications made me really sleepy, but I only took them when the pain got to a point where it was hard to even breathe.

Anyway, back to the real story. I spent most of the early part of my injury on the bed, so when Farhan would leave for work in the morning, he would help me take all my medicine and would take the extra house key and lock the door behind him (This was after I had started standing up and walking a little bit by myself).

This particular morning after he left, I covered my face with the blanket and tried to sleep again. I heard the door close and the key lock behind him. Now, in my mind, I was still awake, and after about 15-20 mins, I heard the front door of the apartment open and hear the click-clack of Farhan's dress shoes as he walked to our room. I realized he must have forgotten something, so I tried to open my eyes, and I couldn't. I can't open my eyes, I can't move my arms, and I can't even lift a finger. As I am trying to move, I hear the click-clack of shoes going to my side of the bed, stopping for 2 seconds and then walking to the other side. I am trying to say Farhan's name but I have no voice, I can't move my mouth! All the while, I listened to the shoes that had stopped on Farhan's side of the bed. Then I hear the change (coins) that Farhan usually left on his bedside table, jingle, like someone is trying to gather them up.

That is when I started panicking! My breathing starts getting erratic, and I finally concentrate and start reading Āyat al-Kursī in my mind (I am definitely awake but I can't move). Halfway through reading Āyat al-Kursī, my arms start moving, my eyes fly open, and I throw off my blanket from my head. I was breathing hard and calling out for Farhan. And! Surprise! Surprise! The house is empty. I immediately messaged him, and yep, he just got to work. Almost in tears, I read all the surahs of protection that I know. Then distract myself by going online.

This happened the next day too, but I had done my research to understand that I was suffering from sleep paralysis. I figured that it was the side effect of one of the stronger meds that I was taking (though it was not mentioned in the leaflet).

The next day when it happened, it was still scary, but I immediately started reading Āyat al-Kursī and broke free of it. It never happened after that, though I continued that medication for a while, but I think it was because my brain realized I knew how to break free of it. But I still can't forget that first morning! It was so real! The click-clack of the shoes I can still hear in my head, and the way the shoes circled my bed and not being able to see or even move a muscle made it even more terrifying.

See! I am a rational person; I don't associate everything with the paranormal, as you all must be thinking by now; I don't try to make everything about scary things. I do all my research, and when I can't find a rational explanation, then it's all supernatural.

Friend or Foe?

This story has always stuck in my mind because it was something that I saw with my own two eyes.

We lived in an apartment about 8 years ago. Now, this apartment was one of the two apartments that we had lived in that had the most activity. We literally saw keys swinging on their own, heard the doors opening and closing, but when we would check, no one would be there, and many other scary disturbances.

BUT nothing beats what happened to me THAT one night.

It was late at night, and we were all asleep. I was sleeping on my left side facing the wall, Farhan was sleeping on my right. From my deep, deep sleep, I suddenly woke up, and just like that, I was wide awake. I was confused as to why this had happened, so I decided maybe turning on my other side would help me sleep.

As I turned, I realized two things:

1) Farhan was facing the other way.

2) There was a black shadow standing at the foot of the bed by Farhan.

I didn't freak out immediately because, duh, it was dark, and I just woke up, and it must just be a shadow. So, I rubbed my eyes and looked again. It hadn't moved! It was still there! A whole human-shaped black shadow! So now I am scared. Too scared to make a sound. I hid my head and literally hid my face on Farhan's back. My breathing got heavier because my heart was racing. I tried to convince myself to look again.

But right then! I hear a faint, 'Madiha'. I froze, obviously, and listened hard. Once again, I hear: 'Madiha'. I jolt up in bed, realizing my mother-in-law is calling me from the other room. I quickly jumped out of bed (hitting Farhan awake), realizing she must not be feeling well. And ran to her room (Shadow forgotten). It turned out her sugar level had dropped so much she couldn't even move from the bed. And she had been trying to call out for help (my Father-In-Law had gone for morning prayers at the mosque), but we were in deep sleep at that time. So afterward, when she was settled and my Father-In-Law had returned from the mosque, we went back to bed. That is when I realized whatever that shadow was, was something that had come to wake me up. Mother-in-law was in danger, and it had wanted to warn us. It scared the living hell out of me, but Alhamdulillah!

This is so prominently ingrained in my mind because I actually saw something! It was so scary. But Alhamdulillah, it was for a good cause, as I like to think of it.

Let's Live Together #1
Bits and Pieces

The last apartment that we lived in was one of the most haunted apartments that we had ever occupied to date! There are many big incidents that took place but the smaller incidents accumulated and painted a scary picture.

Below are some of the things that happened when we first moved in:

Every night there was the sound of a woman crying from a certain corner of my room.

Then there was a time when all of my oven knobs were turned on. My kids were never allowed in the kitchen and they knew that, AND they were watched constantly, so there was no way it could have been them. (This happened at least 3 other times)

Our bed would constantly shake. I thought it was just me, like maybe I had bouts of weakness or something and my body was shaking. But soon enough, Farhan (husband) started feeling it too. One night I actually woke up because of the shaking and it wouldn't stop. I woke up Farhan asking him if he felt it, and soon enough, he realized the bed was actually shaking. It wasn't like the violent shaking that you see in movies but like vibration through the bed.

I started having nightmares, extremely vivid nightmares where I would jerk awake breathing heavily or wake up saying no. Most of the time I didn't remember what I was dreaming of, but sometimes I did. This one 'dream' I still remember to this day.

"The dream starts with me waking up suddenly (like I usually did when I had nightmares but this time, I jerked awake in my dream) and I look at the side of my bed to find my mother-in-law standing, looking down at us. She is just standing there with her head bent a little downwards, arms hanging by her side and hair covering her face. And I called out to her: Is everything ok?

She doesn't reply back. I call her again but she just stands there, and when I start calling her for the third.... all of a sudden something clicks in my brain and I realize, that she isn't supposed to be in the country. We had dropped her at the airport just that morning! And that is when I jolt awake. This is such a real dream for me that I feel like it really happened!"

The TV turns on by itself. And there are many witnesses to this one. My sister, my cousins, mother-in-law, father-in-law, kids, our help, mom, dad etc. Sometimes multiple times throughout the night.

One time our whole fridge was moved up from one side. It looked like someone had taken one side of the fridge and moved it from its place.

This happened ONLY once, but one-night Hamdan (elder son) had a nightmare. In it he saw a HUGE shadow thing in Dada Abu's (grandfather's) room, and he didn't go into their room from that day on. (Thank goodness after that he didn't see anything else.)

We have left lights on in certain parts of our house, only to come back and find all the lights off.

If I listened to music with speakers and not on my headphones, the music would get turned off. Not once but multiple times, till I put my headphones on.

We would hear footsteps when everyone is sleeping, toilets flushing, etc..

All these things and activities were at the extreme when we had first moved in. Before we got, our apartment was blessed. Even afterwards, it's not like these things stopped, but the feeling was less malicious. Though my father-in-law still saw and felt things, he started sharing them less with us, unless it was one of those very extreme things.

But when my FIL passed away, the activity level in the house went down a notch. I can't say it completely stopped, but it went down a lot.

Let's Live Together #2
Buri Shakal

This is just one of the many stories about what happened to my Father-In-Law (Uncle).

Before moving into this apartment, Uncle had gotten sick. He spent the night of our move in the hospital. And after moving, within a week, he was back in the hospital again. He had heart problems and they had gotten pretty bad.

After 2 weeks of being in the hospital, he was discharged.

In that time, I had unpacked the house and everything else was just a blur.

Going to the hospital, cooking, unpacking, elder ones pick and drop to school, and a toddler at home, it was a lot of work.

At night I would fall into bed exhausted.... but rest was hard to come by. I would hear a woman crying from one corner of my room. I used to raise my head and look around and especially to that one corner, only to find nothing. The crying would stop as soon as I raised my head. I would chalk it up to exhaustion and ignore it. It happened at least five times before I could no longer keep my eyes open and go into deep sleep. (It happened almost every night, till we had an Imam Sahab come read Quranic verses in our home.)

Then, when my Father-in-Law was discharged from the hospital, he was very fragile. He could walk on his own but he was very weak. After coming home, he spent most of his time sleeping and praying. He would come out of his room for a little while to have food and to chat with us but then he would return to his room to rest.

One day, I was cleaning my room and I heard Uncle calling my name. And talking in a very loud voice, saying:

Uncle: Kiya chaye apko? Kon hai ap? (What do you want? Who are you?)

I ran to his room quickly to see if everything was OK.

Me: Uncle kon hai? (Uncle who is it?)

Uncle: Yeh kon aurat hai? (Who is this woman?)

(He was sitting up in his bed pointing to the opposite end of the bed)

I quickly crossed over to the other side of the room where my mother-in-law's blanket was, and asked him: Where?

Uncle: Dekho, she is sitting on the corner of the bed!!

I froze at this point.

Uncle: Kitna bura mou banaya hai. (Sitting there with such a terrifying face!)

I moved the comforters around and said: Nahi Uncle yeha koi nahi. (No Uncle, there is no one here)

Uncle: Array woh bethi! Apko nazar kyu nahi arahe! (She is sitting right there; can't you see her?)

Me (terrified but trying to placate him): Uncle shayad comforter aisa houa tha. (Uncle, maybe the blanket is in a weird position, that's why it looks like that.)

By this time, my mother-in-law had come into the room. And she too confirmed there was no one in the room.

My father-in-law just let it go and didn't pursue the topic anymore, muttering: Haan shayad blanket aisay rakha tha. (Yes, maybe it was the blanket)

But he kept staring at the place.

As the days went by, he regularly started complaining about the people in his room.

He would see people sitting on the curtain rod. People walking around his room.

Once he scolded my mother-in-law for not waking up when a woman placed her child next to her while she was sleeping.

He started reading Manzil Dua every day.

One day when he was reading, he looked up and saw a woman sitting on a chair in his room and she looked up at him and showed him her book as well.

He said, it was like she was showing him that I am reading Allah's name too.

For all the logical reader who might think that there might have been something wrong with Uncle's mind etc., upon his own request, we took him to the psychiatrist. Uncle, being a logical man, wanted to rule this out himself. By the end of the session with the psychiatrist, the doctor himself stood up to inform him he was in a perfect mental condition. The doctor being Muslim himself, knew about these other beings and told us to seek out the help of an Islamic scholar.

That is when we brought Imam Sahab and he explained about the beings in our house being good. And my father-in-law was really sensitive to them, especially after his sickness.

Imam Sahab prayed many Quranic verses, and afterwards he said out loud for them (Jins) to stop bothering us as we are all Allah's beings and want to live together in peace. (This is when the woman crying in the corner of my room stopped too.)

Let's Live Together #3
The Voices

This happened within the first year of our move to our last apartment:

My Mother-in-law was admitted to the hospital because her blood pressure was too high. Farhan was staying in the hospital with her. My kids, me and my father-in-law were at home and after our nightly routine of dinner etc., we all retired to our respective bedrooms. That particular night, I took the kids to my room, closed the door and tried to sleep. After the kids had fallen asleep, I picked up my phone and was on it till my eyes started to close from exhaustion and my mind started shutting down. If I had tried to sleep just like a regular person, I would have ended up being scared because I was alone with the kids in the room, so whenever I have to sleep alone, I do the phone trick.

Anyway, that night when my eyes started to close, I heard talking outside of my room.

It was Uncle (FIL) and Farhan's voice........ now I know for a fact Farhan is at the hospital because I had just messaged him and he had told me he was going to sleep IN THE HOSPITAL ROOM!

No way in hell can he be back in the house.... after 5 minutes of him saying goodnight to me!

I hear a whole conversation happening in muttered voices outside my room's door. I can hear clearly that one voice belongs to uncle and the other to Farhan. I lay there frozen, listening, trying to understand what was being said and no, it was not clear at all.

I wanted to go out and see who or what it was... but all of a sudden, clear as day, a thought came to my mind.... "No Madiha, don't do it! That's how they lure you out!" So, against all my instinct to go and check, I didn't go out because I had never heard such a clear thought like that in my head before!

(This was before Imam Sahab had come.)

Needless to say, I did not sleep at ALL that night. The talking did die down after 30mins or so, but O man! That was terrifying!!

Let's Live Together #4
The Crib

It was the weekend. Farhan (husband) and I usually slept late. The kids would sleep latest at 9pm and then Farhan and I would watch a movie together.

The layout of our room is important in this story. It was something like this: as you entered the room on the left side there were 2 chairs and a little table. On the right of the room, we had our bed and attached to the bed was my younger one, Azlan's (younger one), crib. And on the other side of the crib is a wall with windows. We had taken off one of the sides of the crib so it was attached to the bed. There was a little room between our bed and the crib and at night I connected the crib to my bed so that it was easy for me to reach my child during the night.

At that time, Azlan was 2 years old and the elder one, Hamdan, who slept in the bed with us, was 3.

That night, we watched the movie in our bedroom, while the kids slept next to us, and then after turning off the TV (which was right across from the bed on the opposite wall), we settled down.

I was half asleep and half awake. I suddenly heard the crib move.

I thought Azlan was waking up or something. I opened my eyes immediately (as any concerned mother would) but what I saw turned my blood cold! The whole crib jerked to one side. It was as if someone had grabbed one end of the crib and had tried to move it away from our bed. So now the crib is only half attached to the bed and half away from the bed.

I jerked awake and, without a second thought, I grabbed my child from the crib. I took him in my arms and moved him with me in the bed. (I slept right next to the crib at that time).

I turned around wide-eyed to Farhan, who was sitting up too. His were eyes wide open in shock.

I asked him: "DID YOU SEE THAT!?"

Him: Your eyes were closed before. I saw it move a little first time as well. It shook at first and then moved away from the bed.

Me: I am not letting my child sleep there!

Him: Yes! Yes! Of course! Now?

Me: Read all the prayers, Āyat al-Kursī, all of the prayers and go to sleep!

Him: SERIOUSLY!?

Me: What else can we do!?

And believe it or not, within 5 minutes I was sleeping.

Farhan was up for quite a while and told me in the morning that he kept hearing footsteps all around the room. He could not believe I immediately fell asleep! I told him, I completely entrusted my safety to Allah because what else could we do? That's why I slept peacefully. Alhamdulliah.

I never made my kids sleep in the crib again. We changed the setting of the whole room and I gave away that crib as soon as I could!

But it wasn't the crib that was haunted, it was that apartment.

Let's Live Together #5
Overconfidence is Our Downfall

This happened before Coronavirus.

Farhan usually tries to go to the mosque for fajr (morning prayers), so we wake up fairly early. I pray and then go into the kitchen to make breakfast.

Well, this particular morning as Farhan was leaving, he said, "There was a lot of disturbances last night."

OK, before I write down what I said, you have to know that, of course, I have witnessed everything that has happened in our house and believe for sure that there is something supernatural there. But I believe that Farhan is a bit too sensitive to these things. So, in my effort to calm him down, I said:

"It was all fine. There was nothing there last night. People were probably running around in the apartment above us."

He told me not to be so dismissive and try to understand what he was trying to tell me.

But I was being really dumb and I actually said: "Seriously Farhan, there is nothing there, you are being over dramatic."

He said, "OK, I will tell you more after I come back from prayer."

Then he left the house.

I went into the kitchen to make breakfast.

I usually listen to surah Baqarah (Quran) on YouTube on T.V in the morning while I am working in the kitchen. I was making sandwiches and my back was to the microwave and the cupboards. I heard some creaking from behind me. I turned around, but of course nothing was there. In my mind I rationalized it, it was just the cupboards creaking. (Don't ask me why I thought that was a rational explanation). I turned back around and that is when I heard the microwave click and turn on by itself. I just stood there frozen. I was too scared to turn around because I knew there was no one behind me. The kids were sleeping and Farhan had gone to pray.

I started reciting Ayat al Kursī. Still not turning toward the microwave.... that was still on.... then slowly I turned and said, "Ok I am sorry, I know you are here, I won't say that again." (DON'T I sound so brave!) Then turning the microwave off and while reading all the protection prayers, I quickly left the kitchen to wake up the kids.... because it freaked me out a lot!

You might have guessed, by the way I spoke, that I am a bit used to these types of things. But it really scares the hell out of me when these types of things happen.

Then when Farhan came home, I told him and that is when he scolded me and told me to be very careful when I speak. I asked him what he had wanted to tell me.

He said:

"I woke up from the sound of footsteps outside our room. I realized activity had begun. I started reading Ayat Ul Kursī. And started drifting in and out of sleep when I heard the toilet flush in our attached bathroom. That is when I lost all my cool and read everything I could remember."

I was shaken at that point. I mean, it is one thing to hear footsteps and such, but to actually hear the toilet flushing by itself is way too much to handle. Farhan and I stopped discussing these things at home anymore. We would only talk about any incident that he or I had gone through when we were out of the house because from what we could gather, they were always listening and there was no telling what could upset them about our conversation about them.

Please note that we have had Imam Sahab from the masjid nearby come and do some reading in our apartment, but from what we can gather, they are good beings. They also pray to Allah and have their own lives going on. Sometimes it clashes with ours and freaks us out, but they are just living their lives. We asked the Imam Sahab why these types of things happen sometimes. He said, "They are good, but like humans are mischievous, there are some who are the same way.

Insha'Allah they won't cause you any harm but they will prank you guys sometimes."

Let's Live Together #6
It's Walking Down the Hall

Farhan was traveling last December, and when that happens, I usually make one of the kids sleep with me. No way am I sleeping alone in my room. So, the first night Farhan was away was a school night, and I usually slept by 9:30pm because I am always super exhausted on school nights (Yes! I am an old lady). I always put my phone on Airplane Mode before sleeping, so even if I get any messages, they don't get delivered till I turn my phone on, which is usually only in the morning.

I woke up as per usual, at 5am and checked my phone. My live-in helper Hamidah, had sent me 2 messages at around 10:15pm (I was dead asleep by then). Her messages read:

"Madam, are you sleeping?"

"Do you hear the sound of the stick?"

I saw the messages and thought, oh something happened! Hamidah is there to help my mother-in-law out during the night. She sleeps on a separate bed next to my mother-in-law's bed. Hamidah's bed is close to the room's door way.

I waited for her to wake up at around 8am then asked her about her messages that she had sent me.

Hamdiah: Madam! Last night was so scary! I heard a walking stick going up and down the hallway!

Me: What walking stick?

Hamidah: The walking stick that Mama uses! You know, the walking stick makes a certain sound like, "tsh tsh tsh", when my mama uses it?

Me: Yes.

Hamidah: That sound! It would walk to my bed, then stop there, then turn back and walk down the hall again.

Me: Were you sleeping when that happened?

Hamidah: No! I was awake, using my phone. I thought it was mama, maybe she needed to use the bathroom, so I took my headphones off and looked over at her, but she was facing the other way, sleeping.

Me: When you looked over at her, was the stick sound still happening?

Hamidah: Yes madam! I still heard it moving down the hall! After looking at mama, I hid under my blanket! The stick sound then turned around and came towards my bed again. It came up to my bed, stopped and after a little while it turned around and went down the hall! I messaged you then, but I think you were asleep! After 30mins of this happening, I gathered enough guts to stick my head out of the blanket and I looked, nothing was there but I could hear the sounds!

Me: Did you read all the prayers for protection?

Hamidah: Yes, I started praying then. It happened for a long time, but then it stopped at around 12am.

Then I explained to her to beware at night, to pray before lying in bed and to try and sleep along with everyone. She was super freaked but tried laughing it out. I had never spoken to her about this before because I didn't think there was a need for her to be scared from the get-go, but it turned out it's not just our family who felt things in that apartment. The activity was so much there that anyone who lived there or visited us there also had similar experiences to share, even when we had not told them anything about our experiences.

Let's Live Together #7
FROZEN!

That whole week, I hadn't been sleeping well. I don't know why, but I was just extremely disturbed. I would wake up 5-6 times during the night and obviously falling back to sleep after waking up is harder. One of those nights, I was fighting another losing battle with sleep, trying my hardest. I guess I must have slipped intp the state of when you are half asleep but your brain is awake.

When I feel someone grab my ankle, now I'm like, "OK what the hell, let go of my ankle!"

My eyes are still closed as I am trying to shake it off. Then, all of a sudden, both of my legs are being held down by my ankles and I try to wake myself up but I can't, I just can't move, I can't wake up, I can't do anything!!!

I start freaking out even more when I realize I can't yell out either! And in my mind, I started reciting Ayat Al Kursī. And that's when I am released!

My eyes fly open, I'm breathing loudly, and I most definitely wake up Farhan!

He asks me if I had recited all the prayers before sleeping.... I had not...

He said: 'Well, this is the result of that.'

So, obviously, after that day I never forgot to recite my surahs before sleeping.

I swear I can still feel those hands around my ankles, and that helpless feeling of being pinned down.

Let's Live Together #8
Everyone Can Feel IT!

Last year my sister, her husband and daughter were visiting from America and my Khala (aunt) and Khalu (uncle) were visiting from Pakistan. Basically, there were a lot of people in the apartment. My sister, Hina, knows about the story of our house, but my Khala and Khalu don't know anything. Until my Khala (Aunt) had her own experiences there.

I was making food one day and my Khala was standing with me in the kitchen, talking to me. All of a sudden, the pot with the food, started to spin on its own. When I had stirred the food in the pot the last time, it was not in the centre of the stove because I was rushing and distracted while chatting with my Khala. So, this pot literally spins back so that it rests on the centre of the fire, by itself. And my Khala had her eye on the pot because I was busy washing rice and she wanted to make sure that it didn't burn. She says, 'Madiha, did you see that?'

My back was turned away from her and the stove because I was by the sink. I said, "No, what was it?" She told me how the pot had spun and came to sit in the centre of the fire by itself. Then I told her, "Yes Appa (we call her Appa) this is normal and these types of things usually happen in this house." She was surprised at how nonchalant I was and started to ask me for more information.

I told her that many times if I am rushing around or something seems unsafe, things fix itself. Sometimes I don't even notice these things till later on and sometimes these things happen right in front of my face. That pot was basically in a very unsafe position, it could have tipped over or the food could have burned because my back was turned to it, and whatever, it was, made sure that didn't happen.

Once I had forgotten to turn off the stove and I was 100 percent sure that I hadn't, but when I had gone to check in the kitchen, the stove was off. The oven knobs turn by themselves too. My kids are not allowed in the kitchen and they never ever come in by themselves and that was another one of the things. When Appa heard this, she was pretty shocked.

After two days, my Khala also had an encounter of her own. She had gone to the bathroom and when my Khala came out of the bathroom, the door closed by itself and locked. Now these locks aren't your typical press in locks, these are 'twist them all the way around so that they lock' type of locks, and this one locked itself. That really freaked her out. But now my Khala truly has no doubts about the happenings in our house at all!

Hina's Experience:

When Hina and her 2-year-old daughter, Aniyah, were visiting, I would sleep next to Aniyah. Aniyah doesn't sleep next to me, she sleeps on my face, because she is crazy and I love her. Anyway, so while we were sleeping and with her face 2 inches away from mine, I had closed my eyes and all of a sudden, I felt fingers on my arm. With my eyes still closed, I smiled, thinking Aniyah must have put her hand on my arm. But then these two little fingers walked up my arm, up my neck to my face and then all the way up to my head. I thought, "Aww Aniyah is so cute she is playing!", only for my eyes to fly open and realize, Aniyah is one 2! She can't do that! She doesn't know how! And even if she did, she hasn't moved an inch from her spot and her little arms are stuck under her own tummy!

Then I tried to rationalize that it must be Azlan! He must have woken up in the middle of the night, missed me and came to sleep next to me! I looked all around the bed and the room to find no one! And you will not believe that! Three days later, Farhan tells me the same thing happened to him! I hadn't discussed with him what had happened to me, because, honestly, with guests, I hadn't had the time. But then three days later he told me someone had walked their little fingers from his arm to his head! Then I shared with him that the same thing had happened to me too!! Which truly gave us both a scare! We thought about it together, wondering why the activity had picked up so much all of a sudden. The only conclusion we could come up with was that there were too many people in the house and that maybe that caused them to stir even more.

Hina had many experiences on her visit to our house as well. First thing that she noticed were bruises all over her body. These were just random bruises that would appear after the night's sleep. Then another night when she was sleeping, her leg was crooked or bent in a weird position, so something took her leg and straightened it, which truly freaked her out. But as we are all rational beings, she thought she must have been dreaming it. Those rational thoughts all went out the window when, almost every night, something or another would happen to her.

One thing that really scared us were the scratches on Aniyah's face. Aniyah literally didn't have long nails. After her afternoon nap, Aniyah woke up with a scratch running horizontally across her left cheek. It wasn't very deep but it was super long. Hina and I searched the whole bed for anything pointy or sharp but we couldn't come up with an explanation. So we chalked it up something or another. Then, a couple of days later, when the scratch was healing, another scratch appeared, again, after her afternoon nap, and this time running vertically across her cheek. We weren't at all happy to see the scratch in the same area because now it was too much to be just a coincidence! I told Hina to read all the surahs of protection that she knew whenever Aniyah slept alone and, of course, to which she replied she already does. But, Alhamdulliah after that, she didn't get scratched again, but to be fair, two times was one too many.

On the last night, Hina, Aniyah and I slept together, because after her husband had come, I had given the family the room and slept with my kids. So that night we were all just really disturbed. Aniyah kept moving around, I wasn't able to go into deep sleep, and Hina just could NOT sleep. After a little while, Hina shook me awake, and I was shocked because, literally, in all the years that we have been alive, she has never ever woken me up! I was always the scaredy cat who would try to keep her awake after watching a scary movie because I wouldn't be able to sleep. I told her not sleep on your back and to turn on her right side and sleep. She told me that she was sleeping on her side. I asked her what was wrong. She said, "I feel the bed shaking", so I just say oh and told her to read all the prayers for protection and Ayat al Kursī and to keep reading them till she fell asleep. She turned towards me, and closed her eyes. I reached over Aniyah and put my hand on her face and slowly patted her in a reassuring sort of a way so that she would know I was there while she slept.

She did eventually drift off to sleep, but then soon she was shaking me awake again. She was super scared and she was so scared that she was going to go and wake up her husband, which is another first because Masha 'Allah, Hina and sleep are best friends. Somehow, I managed to calm her down and we slept till fajr. In the morning, I asked her what had happened. She told me she saw a light at the foot of our bed where there wasn't even a hint of light. She said she saw that there was bright light, which I thought was OK, because lights are usually associated with positive things. But then she said there was something standing right next to her, which truly did freak me out too. So he kept waking up and kept feeling something or another. Thankfully, that was her last night in the apartment because they had a flight to catch.

Story from Saudi Arabia

By: Madiha Khan

The Shared Hotel Room

When we went for hajj, we had reached Kaaba late at night. Farhan, my Mother-In-Law, and I had gone together to Saudi Arabia for this amazing journey. My Mother-In-Law was in the wheelchair and, since it had been a long flight and a long trip to our hotel, we had decided to rest till fajr before going to the Kaaba for Tawaf.

The room that we were allotted was truly a piece of work. It was a normal looking room, packed with all the luxuries a person could want, in a famous hotel right-in the haram limits. There were three beds in the room and all three of us (Farhan, mother-in-law, and I) were in each of our separate beds. We all went to sleep almost immediately, but in the middle of the night, all of a sudden, I was alert.

As I realized I was awake, I tried to figure out why I was so suddenly aware of my surroundings, without opening my eyes. I had a feeling that I shouldn't open my eyes at all and should just drift back to sleep. But I wanted to put my "irrational" fear at ease and wanted to prove to myself that I was just scaring myself for no reason. As I opened my eyes, I realized that the lamp across the room was on. It was a table lamp, nothing too big, so it wasn't overly bright. I realized we had turned off all the lights of the room before sleeping, except the one by the bathroom for my mother-in-law to be able to use it during the night. We had had a whole discussion on this matter before sleeping, so there was no way I was mistaken or misremembering it!

As I was still trying to figure out the lamp issues, I realized I was also seeing 2-3 men in ihram, rushing around the room, specifically near the lamp area, which obviously didn't make sense. This room belonged to three of us and unless someone broke in our room there was no one else but us three there. I heard them murmuring to each other and rushing about, trying to leave as quietly and quickly as they could. Then I realized another thing: I couldn't really make out their faces. No matter how much I tried to concentrate on their faces, they just weren't clear, they looked as if someone had blurred them out.

I was lying there as still as I could manage too, not wanting them to discover that I was awake. I didn't know what to do, all I could think of was to read Ayat al Kursī, and I started reciting it. I shut my eyes for two minutes. As I finished reading Ayat al Kursī, I opened my eyes and...

They were gone....

I told Farhan the next morning about what had happened and he said, "It makes sense because even Jinnat have to do hajj, so we must be sharing the room with them."

This did give me some clarity on the matter, but it was really scary seeing some random men in our room late at night!

But, Alhamdulliah, after that night, I was so exhausted after each day of Tawaf and Salah that I didn't feel anything and just dropped into dreamless sleep each night.

Stories from Pakistan

By: Madiha Khan

A Consistent Entity
Part 1

When my parents had gotten married, my mom had moved into my dad's family home with him in Karachi, Pakistan. It was a huge house for a huge family. My dad had 10 brothers and sisters. Most of the sisters had already gotten married by the time my mom came into the story, but there were still some brothers who were unmarried, because they were finishing their studies or had just started working. My grandparents obviously lived there as well. As the years flew by, most of the brothers either settled in the States or out of Karachi. My Dada (grandfather) passed away after my sister and I were born. Soon my mom and dad lived there only with our Dadi (grandmother), with regular visits from all the sisters who lived around the area.

One of my dad's sisters had to relocate from Saudi Arabia back to Karachi, Pakistan, so until they were able to find a home of their own, they moved in with our family in the family house. My Phopo (Aunt) has 7 kids, and the eldest was already married, and all of these cousins of ours were older than us. We were super excited when they came and started living with us and soon, we had all fallen into a routine. But as time went on, my older cousins started complaining about a man in a white shalwar kameez They would usually see him in the backyard, or the alleyways that led to the backyard, or the parking garage, or on the terrace. They would catch glimpses of white out of the corner of their eyes, or see a figure standing in the corner and then when they would look again, no one would be there.

Once, my mom and us kids had gone to our Nani's house and my cousins had come home early after their college had finished for the day. They knew my mom wasn't home and that the house was locked up, but they heard people talking inside. They were really confused, so they moved back away from the front gate to look at the top part of the house only to see a figure in white just going around the corner on the roof of the house! They got scared and went to the neighbours to call my mom to confirm if she was still at my Nani's place, which she was. They thought maybe someone had broken in, and they spent some time at the neighbours till their brothers came home to check but no one was there (don't ask me why the police weren't called).

Then this became a regular thing, flashes of white, talking etc. My mom, who had been living in that house for over 7-8 years, now dismissed all this, saying it's all paranoia. She always said she has been living there the longest and she has neither heard nor seen anything. My Dadi, who was always there too, confirmed what my mom said and didn't take all of this too seriously. One late night at around 2am, our doorbell rang, we barely stirred, and then it kept ringing insistently, till my Baba woke up panicked, rushing to answer the door. He found our neighbour across the street standing there frantic! The neighbour told us we needed to immediately leave the house! He said he saw a man in a white shalwar kameez sitting on the roof of our house and as he was watching him, the man suddenly disappeared! He was scared that it was an intruder or something and helped my Baba search the house, but obviously there was nothing there.

My sister and I could never sleep in our own room. The room that was ours had long windows that covered 2 walls of the bedroom. One part of the windows overlooked the terrace and the other faced the alleyways leading to the back of the house. I was always scared in that room without any rational reason. I never saw anything or heard anything, but I always felt so scared that it was unbearable. To this day I can still recall that insane fear that used to grip me, and God forbid, I would ever wake up in the middle of the night! I would run to my parent's room every single time! My parents got so sick of our behaviour that they would just put an extra bed in their bedroom where we could sleep.

Remember when I told you about my mom not believing anything?!

Well, after a phone call to my other Phopo, where she proclaimed very loudly that it was all nonsense what the others said, about this house.... She got a wakeup call. Let me also make this clear, by this time, my cousins and Phopo had moved out, my Baba was in the States for work and my Dadi was visiting her elder son in the States too, so my mom and us kids use to live alone in that house. Some of our older guy cousins would come over to stay the night, so that we wouldn't be all alone in that huge house. So that night when my mom went to bed (we were sleeping next to her), she felt pressure on her chest and hands around her throat as if something was choking her. Her eyes flew open and she saw a figure in white sitting on her chest with its face, which really wasn't a face but just a shadow, close to hers, saying: 'Dekh! Tu kheti hai na mei nahi hou! Mei hou!!' (Look! You tell everyone I am not here! HERE I AM!)

She started reciting Ayat al Kursī, and soon the pressure was off her chest and the fingers around her throat loosened. There was a loud banging and yelling from outside, and forgetting her fear, she ran to see what was happening outside. As she entered the TV lounge, she saw 3 of my cousins rushing outside. One had a cricket bat in his hand, another a huge knife and the last one had an iron rode (don't ask me why we even had that). They all went out of 3 different exits of the house only to meet in the backyard. When, at last, they came back in, and they told my mom they saw a man in white running from the terrace to the alleyway towards the back part of the house. That is when they had all taken up weapons to catch this man, only to find nothing. There was no way for this man to escape because they all literally came at him from all the possible exits. This truly freaked my mom out and she never spoke up about such things so freely, figuring she must have upset whatever it was. She had never been disturbed by this thing but when she kept saying boldly: 'kuch nahi hai, kuch nahi hai, mei kab sai reh rahe hou!' (There is nothing there, I have been living here for so long, I haven't seen anything!) she must have really upset this thing.

A Consistent Entity
Part 2

My mom told me about one another incident. Actually, I saw this myself, with my own eyes in fact! I was part of this:

I was in my room (the same room I could never sleep in) playing and all of a sudden, I heard my little sister Maha, who was 10-11 months at that time, screaming and crying her head off. I had never heard her crying this way before and even though I was only 9, I knew something was wrong. So, I yelled for my mom, asking her what was going on!? She cried out for me to come quickly! I thought Maha had fallen down somewhere and hurt herself and my mom needed my help. I went running to my mom's room where I had heard her calling me from.

The layout of my room is different. When you entered her bedroom, the bed was right next to the entry door facing the wall filled with windows and a door leading to the back part of the house where the clothes were washed. When I got there, my mom was on the bed facing the windows and Maha in her lap. I saw my mom trying to calm Maha down while she looked towards the windows, screaming and crying her head off. My mom was trying to make her face away from the window but she was thrashing wildly in her arms looking at the windows area of the room. The reason why my mom didn't just get up and leave the room was because my mom has always been a petite woman and Maha was a big baby, and the way she was going crazy in her lap, it would have been impossible for my mom to safely carry her off the bed.

I asked my mom what was happening as I entered the room, though I could see Maha was freaking out while looking at the window, which freaked me out too! My mom yelled for me to close the curtains of the room and to close the door that led to the back part of the house. I am a scaredy-cat and was getting scared going near the windows! But my mom's angry yells for me to do it spurred me forward and I quickly closed the curtains and the door. Almost instantly, Maha calmed down, and while hiccupping she settled with her head on my mom's shoulder. I obviously glued myself to mom's side while she read all the protection prayers to keep us safe.

Another thing I remember very clearly was a reoccurring nightmare that I used to have in that house. In this nightmare I would be running at full speed from the terrace to the back alley (the same alley that overlooked my bedroom) and there are a million snakes chasing me. In my head I would be thinking about how to escape them, only to realize that snakes can literally climb on walls and even go in water. All of sudden, there is a tree in the alleyway and I climb that tree while freaking out because I know in a few minutes the snakes will start climbing the tree. And that is when I would wake up! I had this dream many times and I even had it once or twice after I moved to the States.

A Consistent Entity
Part 3

After we moved to the States, the house was put up for rent and a family with a little girl came to live there. Within a few months, the man of the family had passed away. Apparently, he had some undetected disease that flared up and he died. After a month or two of his passing, my mom was visiting Pakistan and wanted to have a look at the house. So she got the lady's number and set up a day to visit. When she went to the house, she saw that the little girl was only 6 years old and was playing by herself. The lady was sad, but had accepted her husband's passing. She showed my mom around the house. My mom had severe nostalgia while walking around the house as she had spent a good 10 years there.

After she had looked around, she sat with the lady for tea. While they had tea, the lady asked more about my mom and her time in the house. My mom told her fond memories and funny stories of her time there. The lady pushed my mom for more, but my mom didn't realize what she was trying to ask and kept on telling her good memories and stories. Then my mom asked her about her life, husband, and daughter. This was the lady's cue and she got really serious. She asked my mom to answer one question for her and that too honestly. My mom said she would try her best, then she asked her if there was anything in the house. My mom looked her straight in the eye and said, yes there was, and asked her what had happened to her there. This is when my mom wanted to test her and see what she had experienced was the same as what we had experienced.

Without hesitation, the lady launched into her story:

"As soon as they had moved into the house, their financial standing started to decline and they suffered a loss in their business. Which is a very normal thing and since this family was not superstitious, they did not associate it with their, move, ups and downs happen in business. Then her husband's health started to decline. At first, they thought it was because of the stress that he was taking because of the loss in business. Then one day he collapsed and was rushed to the hospital, where he was diagnosed with a rare disease which he didn't have a chance to survive and within months he was gone.

While all this was going on, the daughter had started playing with an imaginary friend. She used to have little tea parties with the 'friend', she used to speak to the 'friend' in whispers, she used to want to do everything with this 'friend'. The elders thought, because of all the problems in the house, she wasn't getting much attention, so she had decided to make up a friend. But soon the whispers turned into full on talking and she would be talking to this friend all the time. She would ask for permission from this friend to do everything, she would wake up in the middle of the night and walk out of the room, and when asked why, she would say her friend was calling her. Sometimes things would disappear and the girl would know the exact location of it. For example, once the rolling pin disappeared from the kitchen, and the lady looked everywhere but could not find it. She was truly baffled because how in the world could a rolling pin disappear, while she was making chapatti!?! While the lady was searching for the rolling pin and her daughter came into the kitchen. She skipped to her mom and told her, "I know what you are looking for!" The lady was already irritated because she wanted to finish her work, but it was hindered because of the missing rolling pin. So she told her daughter, "Love, I am busy, please go out and play." The little girl then ran to the kitchen door and got the rolling pin out from behind the door and showed it to her shocked mom. The lady could not understand how it could have gotten behind the kitchen door and how her daughter knew what she was looking for. She just scolded her daughter for playing a prank on her and shooed her out of the kitchen.

After a couple of months of this happening, the lady started to suspect paranormal involvement. Her daughter was relying on the unseen friend constantly for comfort, companionship, and consolation and she had started disappearing around the house for long periods of time. Soon her daughter started getting sick. The lady spoke to her daughter seriously about her friend. Her daughter described the friend as a tall thin man, who wore a white shalwar kameez. The lady had thought that her daughter had imagined a little boy or a girl her own age, not a full-grown man. This description had alarm bells ringing in her head and she quickly asked her daughter where this man lived. The little girl looked at her mom, then grabbed her hand and took her into the kitchen. Then she pointed up to the little crawl space in between the kitchen ceiling and the cabinets. "There, mama, he lives there!'"

As she finished her story my mom sat there looking at her in disbelief! She was stunned! She knew that our family had been through some experiences but it had never been this extreme! This was too much! And my mom told the lady as much too. She told her she needed to move out as soon as possible because we had never suffered to this extent and her case was totally messed up. The lady already knew this and had already given her notice period to the home owners. And thankfully she was able to move out without any harm to her daughter. She had already lost her husband, but to lose her daughter would have been unbearable for her.

That house is still there. Later it was turned into a school. That also didn't survive either. Now the bottom part of the house still stands empty and only the upper part is in use by the main owners of the home.

Glossary

A

Abbu: Dad

Alhamdulillah: An Arabic phrase meaning "praise be to God", sometimes translated as "thank God".

Ammi: Mom

Appi: Respectful way to address older sister

Āyat al-Kursī: is one of the strongest means of protection from the devils

Azan/Adhaan: Muslims call for prayer

B

Baba: Dad

Bhaiya: Respectful way to address older brother

Buri Shakal: Scary Face

C

Chotu ka Chai Stall: Chotu's Tea Stall

Churail: A witch. A woman who is believed to have magic powers, especially evil ones.

D

Dada Abu's: Grandfather (Dad's side)

Dadi: Dad's mom. Grandmother.

Duas: Prayers

Dupatta: Scarf

F

Fajr: this prayer is the first of the five mandatory salah (Islamic prayer), to be performed anytime starting from the moment of dawn and before the sunrise.

G

Ghagharas: Indian skirts

H

Haram: Masjid al-Haram also known as the Grand Mosque or the Great Mosque of Mecca, is a mosque enclosing the vicinity of the Kaaba in Mecca.

I

In sha Allah: God willing

Ihram: Men's ihram clothing consists of two white cloths, without seams, hems or buttons.

Imam Sahab: a learned teacher or doctor of Islamic law

J

Jinnat: what the race of Jins are called. According to Islam, jinn are supernatural beings made by God. Jinn are made of fire, like humans were made of clay.

Jinns/Jin/Jins/Jinn: a magical spirit who may appear in the form of a human or an animal and can take control of a person.

K

Kaaba: also spelled Ka'ba, Ka'bah or Kabah, sometimes referred to as al-Ka'ba al-Musharrafa, is a stone building at the centre of Islam's most important mosque and holiest site, the Masjid al-Haram in Mecca, Saudi Arabia

Khala: Mother's sister. Aunt.

Khalu: Mother's sister's husband. Uncle.

L

Lambani: Peddler

M

Masha 'Allah: is an Arabic phrase that means, in its literal sense, that 'Allah has willed it [has happened].

Manzil Dua: is used for protection from several factors which include Ruqyah from black magic, jinn, witchcraft, sorcery, evil eye and so forth.

Methi bajra puri/aloo sabzi: Indian Food

Moulvi: a learned teacher or doctor of Islamic law

N

Nani: Maternal Grandmother.

P

Paan: Betel Leaf

Paranda: a women's hair ornament made of multi-coloured silk threads and decorated with floral (bunches) designs and ornamental tassels

Peer Saab: a learned teacher or doctor of Islamic law

Phopo: Dad's sister. Aunt.

Puris and Kheer: Pakistani/Indian Food

R

Ruqyah Centre: Ruqyah in Islam is the recitation of Qur'an, seeking of refuge, remembrance and supplications that are used as a means of treating sicknesses and afflictions such as:

- Black Magic
- Jinn Possession
- Evil Eye

S

Salah: The Arabic term for the ritual prayer that is obligatory for Muslims to perform five times a day.

Subhan Allah: The simple act of reciting Subhan Allah is a way to glorify Allah. To show your appreciation and be grateful for all the blessings he's bestowed in your life.

Surah Baqarah: the second chapter of Quran. Its major benefit is that it protects you from Shaitan (Satan). Reciting surah al-Baqarah daily will protect us from anyone who wishes us harm, the evil eye, and witchcraft.

Surah Rehman: part of the holy book, Quran.

Surah: Chapter in the sacred scripture of Islam, the Quran.

T

Tawaf: the act of walking in circles the Holy Kaaba seven times in an anti-clockwise direction.

U

Umrah: The Umrah is an Islamic pilgrimage to Mecca that can be undertaken at any time of the year.

Stories By:

*Madiha Khan
*Geet Bhambra
*Samina Namoji
*Syeda Aumme Salma
*Shaheen Razack
*Amrin Siddique
*Aisha Sultana
*Saba M.Bashir
*Aatqa Ali
*Ashrafunnisa S. Zameer
*Rashida Aliasgar Darukhanawala
*Adeela Mushtaq

About the Author

Madiha Khan

Madiha Khan is a small-time blogger from Dubai, UAE. She was born in Pakistan, but grew up in Illinois, USA. A teacher by profession but an artist at heart, Madiha has always been trying to find and share the beauty around her with others. She loves to eat really spicy food, hanging out with her family and reading. She currently lives with her husband, kids and Mother-in-law in an apartment in Dubai, and looks forward to new adventures life brings her each day.

www.ingramcontent.com/pod-product-compliance
Lightning Source LLC
LaVergne TN
LVHW041849070526
838199LV00045BA/1506